Grounds for SUSPICION

Vol.V of Indian Creek Anthology Series

© 1998 Southern Indiana Writers

ISSN 1085-357X

Grounds For Suspicion
Volume 5 of the Indian Creek Anthology Series

Second Edition

Published by Southern Indiana Writers, 2200 Reno Ave., New Albany, IN, 47150
Book designed by T. Lee Harris

ISSN 1085-357X
ISBN 978-0-6152-0353-9

Cover Art and design by T. Lee Harris

First Edition 1998
Second Edition 2008

Contents

The Absolution
by Glenda Mills

St. Dymphna's Asylum stood white and stark against the dark trees and deep green grass of the countryside. Blotches of red, yellow, and purple grew scattered in flower beds along the walks. The whole setting was lovingly tended. The Sisters of Charity made sure of that. Father William, however, found no inspiration in its beauty. As he slowly made his way up the steps, he thought about the Pharisees Jesus rebuked, comparing them to whitewashed tombs which were attractive to look at but, inside, were filled with the stench of death. The holy oil used to anoint him during his ordination barely had time to soak in, and already he dreaded his duties at St. Dymphna's because here he was surrounded by people whose spirits had been hulled out, leaving behind empty shells in a suspended state of lifeless existence. Tightening his grip on his leather bag, he squared his shoulders against the chill in his heart and finished climbing the steps, stopping halfway up to catch his breath and rest his tired legs.

When he opened the heavy wooden door at the top, the chill in his heart swept over his entire body, leaving goose bumps down his arms. There on the wall facing him was the picture, a very large antique rendition of St. Dymphna kneeling in prayer. She was meant to be an inspiration to the patients, a reminder that someone in Heaven was praying for them, but as he gazed into the oily colors, his imagination once again took him beyond the depiction of the prayerful child to her death, a death that came at the hands of her own father. He saw with grisly clarity the slashing knife, the girl's head hanging from her father's hand, blood gushing from her severed neck and a wave of nausea overtook him. He had to swallow hard to keep from gagging.

"Good morning, Father." Sister Mary Teresa's voice was joyful and bright, pulling Father William from the horrifying darkness of the painting. He nodded, trying to return the woman's smile. It was a weak attempt at best, but it was enough to appear polite.

After signing in, he walked quickly down the hall, glancing up occasionally to make note of a room number before returning his gaze to the backs of his folded hands. He nodded to the people he met, avoiding eye contact. He was greatly relieved when he finally arrived at room 111.

According to Sister Mary Teresa, the woman in the bed before him had been here some twenty years. No one knew much about her except that she'd been found wandering a small country road in the area, no identification, no local relations, nothing. To complicate matters further, she had not spoken a word in all that time. When no physical cause for her muteness could be determined, she was sent here to live out her life in silence, but now her life was coming to an end.

The woman did not stir when he entered the room. For a moment, he thought he might be too late, but then he saw the cotton blanket rise and fall slightly. Carefully, he unpacked his stole, kissed it, and placed it around his neck. He put the bottle of holy oil on the table beside the bed. The good sisters had already placed a crucifix, two lit candles, a bottle of holy water and a spoon on the table in preparation for the final sacrament. Since it was obvious there would be no confession to hear, Father William took the holy water and sprinkled it on the woman. He used a spoon to gently place a small piece of host on her tongue, and laid his hands on her head in silence. Putting oil on his thumb, he anointed her forehead and hands.

"Daughter of God, through this holy anointing may the Lord in His love and mercy help you with the grace of the Holy Spirit. May the Lord who frees you from sin save you and raise you up."

He actually smiled as he began to put his things away. This hull would soon be reunited with her essence, and in that reunion she would find her voice, a voice more beautiful than any she could have known before. Death for her and for so many in this God-forsaken place was the only chance they had for life, untormented, free and eternal.

"Father, forgive me, for I have sinned."

Her voice was low and raspy, barely more than a whisper, but it echoed in the silence of that small room like distant thunder on a sultry summer evening. Father William turned around on unsteady legs, trying not to spill the holy oil in his trembling hands. The woman hadn't moved. Her eyes were closed, her face toward the ceiling.

Careful, Will, he said to himself. *Don't let this place work its cursed spell on you too.* His admonishment steadied his nerves, and he once again turned away from the bed to pack his bag.

"Father, forgive me, for I have sinned."

Her voice was stronger this time, imploring him to respond. He sat down on the side of the bed and placed his hand on her shoulder.

"Speak, my child, for I am listening." His voice was as unsteady as hers.

For a moment the woman said nothing, and he wondered if he had heard the final rambling of a tortured soul on its way to redemption. Just as he raised his hand to pronounce absolution, the woman spoke again.

"I am a young woman, married. My husband is good to me at first, takes care of me, loves me. Then things change, late nights at work, business trips out of town, playing cards all night. I suspect but I never ask. I don't want to know."

Her eyes were closed. Her bottom lip quivered slightly, and he felt her shoulder relax with her sigh.

"Then one day I see him at a little coffee shop downtown, someone else with him, laughing, touching, kissing. I run home and find it all in his desk, letters, pictures, divorce papers." The tremor in her bottom lip increased and intermittent tears ran down the side of her face into her graying hair.

We know how this game plays out, don't we Will? How many times, old friend, have we watched the heartbreak? Oh, but there was that one time, that one very special time. We remember, don't we? Of course we do. How could we ever forget? A sob caught in his throat, but he cleared it away.

"I don't know what to do." The woman paused. "I want to hurt him, make him pay. I blow out all the pilot lights, turn on the burners and leave, waiting in a park across the street. God forgive me. I wait for him to come home."

Yes, Lord, forgive us. Forgive us even though we cannot forgive ourselves. We had a past too, didn't we, Will? Before we got our mid-life calling.

"I hear the car stop, look toward the house, want to see him one last time, but it's not his car. I try to scream. She can't hear me."

The woman's voice had risen to a wail. Heavy sobs arched her frail body off the bed and tears flowed in a steady stream now.

"I hide, so frightened. The fire, the smoke, the sirens. What have I done? Precious Jesus, what have I done?" The wailing gave way to deep, choked sobs.

Do you remember, Will, what a fire is like? We watched everything go up before our eyes, as if Hell itself had opened its vile jaws in all its fury and devoured everything and everyone in judgement against us. We paid a costly price, didn't we, my friend? The sins of the father visited on the children.

Father William pulled a worn black breviary from his jacket pocket. He was not interested in the prayers it contained. Instead, he opened the cover carefully and stared at the small photograph taped inside. A twelve-year-old girl with long, dark hair smiled back at him. He closed his eyes and time became a twister spinning wildly, images whirling in blurred chaos, leaving his life a confused pile of rubble before dissipating. He shook his head abruptly trying to rearrange the pieces.

The woman's sobs gradually began to subside. He wasn't sure if she really knew he was even there, but it didn't matter. The look on her face softened as blessed exhaustion came and calmed her. As she lay there once more peaceful and quiet, Father William again extended his right hand to grant absolution, but before he could say a word, an apparition appeared beside the woman's bed, a twelve-year-old girl with long, dark hair. She looked at him and smiled.

He stood there staring at the girl— for how long he did not know. It wasn't until his breviary slipped from his trembling hands and hit the floor that time became a reality again.

"It can't be. My God, it just can't be." His voice leaked out in a thin, stunned whisper. He turned his gaze toward the woman in the bed. After twenty years of being bedridden, the color was gone from her cheeks. She'd lost a lot of weight. Her hair had turned from auburn to gray. It was short now, asylum rules required it. Her face was thin and drawn. He still could not see the color of her eyes, but he knew they were green, the most beautiful unique shade of green he'd ever seen.

"All this time, I thought you were dead." The initial shock quickly gave way to rage, a rage Father William had not known since the fire,

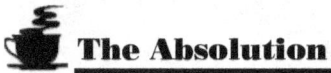

the fire that killed his daughter. "It was you. You killed her." The words hissed through clenched teeth. He started toward the bed, his hands knotted into tight fists, but twenty years of anger, guilt, and despair turned his knees to rubber. He collapsed on the floor, deep wrenching sobs convulsing his body.

As he sat on the floor crying into his hands, he felt the warmth of her touch on his shoulder, a touch that quieted his mind and body and healed his tormented soul. He looked up into his daughter's soft brown eyes, saw her smiling at him, and found peace, something he had not known for such a long time.

The girl left him, walked to her mother's bedside, and took the wrinkled hand in hers. Then she disappeared. The rhythmic rise and fall of the blanket stopped. Their absolution was complete.

Hearts In Spades
by Marian Allen

When I am as old as the rose in my hand
(comparatively, not exactly),
I'll think of your falseness and I'll understand
and see it all matter-of-factly.

You didn't observe, when you ravished my prize,
the gap that was left by your gleaning?
I knew my own blooms on her table. Her eyes
met yours with such passionate meaning...

And you told us both you had business out West
in Reno. (Oh, weren't you clever?)
Divorce was an option, but my way was best—
Lose you to that bubble-brain? Never!

How wild we both were when you didn't return!
How crushed, when they said you'd deserted!
But, unlike your doll, I have money to burn
and know your escape was averted.

My evenings are spent, now, in town at The Grind,
in coffee and free conversation.
I take them bouquets and I open my mind
        on organic fertilization.

Scenes from a Murder
by Dirk Griffin

scene i

inhale warmth
the crowd
companions
richness consumed
among conversation
espresso and latté

taste darkness
on your lips
burnt bitter sweet
watching white flakes
drift beyond the
windowed haven

hear silence
falling between
words
between breaths
between moments
today

touch life
softly in smiles
exchanged
moments taken

lost
remembered
sought

see today
through all
days spent
drinking
hearing
touching
silence
sweetness
darkness
words
moments

A Matter of Morals
by Joy Kirchgessner

Inside a tiny jail cell Matt Loyde lay face upward on the complimentary steel cot, hands cupped behind his head. His attention was on a roach crossing the ceiling. *The very icon of filth,* he thought to himself, *just like she was, just like they all are. Whore, roach...what's the difference? Oh yes, Mom always preached, "Whores are blemishes on the face of the earth." After all, according to her one had lured Pop away. I remember when she caught me with a girlie magazine. She recited "The Ten Commandments" while she sliced a cross in the palm of my hand with a razor blade over the bathroom sink. Said she was "castin' out the demons." What was I...ten, eleven years old maybe. Still have a faint scar.* He surveyed the compact cell walls. *Spent many a day and night locked in a smaller room than this cell. The closet in the basement was Mom's favorite for punishment. That damp, dirty place where I was to "repent and think about my sins." What light there was filtered through the louvered door. Saw a lot of you big ugly brown bastards down there.*

The roach hesitated at the edge of the florescent light.

Well, isn't that where all prostitutes traditionally like to stand? My little bug preferred the pole lights of the interstate rest stops. The little pull-offs for the weary travellers where all the ones like her, ever so fondly known as beavers, like to make their "dates" with the truckers via CB radio. Her voice... something about her screeching country-bumpkin-voice told me she was the one. Been listening to her and watching her for weeks for the right moment. Had a special spot in the woods at the rest stop picked out just for us. Even cut the security fence ahead of time. Cut it so we could close it behind us. Didn't want to be disturbed. Waited till she was through keeping company with the trucker in the big red tractor. Finally, she climbed down from his cab. I could see her beneath the pole lights. She was all dressed up in denim shorts, cowboy boots, a tight knit sweater that emphasized her two bouncing homegrown melons, and a western scarf tied round her neck to top off the cowgirl hooker ensemble. For a little extra money, honey, one more John didn't matter. Where didn't matter, either; she followed me willingly. Oh, I was every bit the gentleman: helping her through the fence and guiding her by the hand to just inside the cover of the woods. We lay down on the dry, dead leaves that crackled with our weight.

"Show Momma what you got," she said with that grating voice so familiar somewhere in the back of my mind. I strangled her with her own scarf. She thought it was all part of the game...until it was too late. I couldn't see her face clearly in the moonlight. Didn't want to. Just wanted to feel her beneath me struggling for freedom. Squeezed her neck until her vile soul popped out like pus from a pimple.

The image of his mother's face interrupted the scene. The thought made him stiffen and go blank for a moment.

The roach zigzagged down the wall past the surveillance camera.

Good thing those cameras can't take pictures of the inside of a person's head. He chuckled to himself. *What a show that would be. Don't you think so you ugly brown...hey where did that thing go?*

The roach made its way across the floor and stopped at the entrance to the cell.

"Up and at 'em, Officer Loyde," a friendly voice summoned from the hall just outside the cell. "Can't run around all night and sleep all day. Your shift starts in about fifteen minutes. Don't see how you can nap in a cell anyway. Have you taken a really good look at some of the characters we have to lock up in these places?"

"I'm up. I'm up, 'Officer' Phillips since you seem to be in a formal mood this morning. If you were as tired as I was, you'd sleep anywhere, too."

Phillips peered around the door and offered, "There's fresh hot coffee and doughnuts in the break room."

"Breakfast of champions. Be right there," Officer Matt Loyde replied as he got up off the cot, tucked in his shirt tail, combed his hair and straightened his badge. As he approached the cell door, he saw the roach and ground it into the floor with the toe of his shoe. "Just how I like it, fresh and hot." Then he thought to himself, *Maybe I should go visit Mom.*

Café au Lait
by Jeannine Baumgartle

I watch
behind bars, hands gripping
square steel, as the guard
tips his steaming mug
for a scald of coffee,
sits back, settles,
sucks the flavor
from his lips, indifferent
to prisoners boring hate
into his uniformed shoulder;
see Them too,
my old friends
at the coffee house,
pleasant, chatty, over their
espresso, their café au lait,
their latté and cappuccino,
hate the pleasure they
take from the drink
with its heady aroma,
provoking sensations,
a dark black thirst,

the liquid weight
lifted to slake it
bites, bitter, hot,
souring expectations,
still, forced to endure
the camaraderie, the satisfaction
of everyone else as they
stir and smile and lick
the ends of spoons, tasting
pleasure I can't experience,
sweep from the table
in one stroke,
laps full of
hot cream and sugar
and dripping blackness
like blood–
for which I am
here, watching
the dull policeman
quietly fueling
my covert fury

Scenes From a Murder
by Dirk Griffin

scene ii

she brings smiles drifting through the door
dark coat dropping reveals
pastel scarf and simple dress
a rainbow slowly moving
from the cold
a song laughing gently

dusky short hair
full deep eyes
lips red and shining

conversing here she
leaves behind her other world
facile friends
expensive cars
exclusive clubs
elusive lies

java jive
java alive
she embraces
living
she embraces
loving

exchanging money
for a
rich and
steamy
dutch almond mocha

Bones

by T. Lee Harris

Most people think of bones as gleaming white. A lot of years with the FBI taught me different and these café au lait hollow orbits staring up at me from the Kentucky clay were no exception. Café au lait was an ironic description, too, since these remains were found under the cellar floor of what was once a coffee shop. At least that's what the sign on the window had said before the building had been razed. From what I'd heard, coffee was only *one* import available in that place— and the only legal one.

Not that I'd ever been in the place. It closed down in the mid-Eighties— long before I came to Louisville, but its reputation survived the business. From the grisly memento emerging from the construction crater for the new Burgess Insurance Tower, seemed like it was surviving the building that housed it, too.

"So you gonna stare at her all day, or you gonna tell me what you think?"

I wrenched my gaze away from the dead sockets and turned to the cop at my side. I answered: "What I think, Levitz, is I want to know why you wanted me down here. I'm not with the Bureau anymore, remember?" Levitz didn't respond except to hunch farther into his coat against a gust of cold wind. I turned and walked up the side of the excavation, letting the forensic anthropologists and photographers get back to their task.

After a moment, Levitz followed. Once on the sidewalk, he glowered into the slate-gray sky and bellowed into the crater: "You guys better haul ass, looks like it's gonna start snowin' any minute." Then he smacked my sleeve as he plodded past me and on across the blocked street, saying: "I'm a two hundred pound copsicle. C'mon, let's get a cappuccino or somethin' across the street; it's a new place, but it's pretty good."

It was warm inside and smelled of fresh coffee and hot pastry, but

that did little against the coldness inside me. Remains like those in the construction site behind us were one of the reasons I left the Bureau. It was hard to take anonymous cases like this; harder if you knew their names. I still wake up screaming sometimes. Out of self defense, I got back to business, maybe a little harsher than needed: "Dammit, Levitz, you still haven't told me why I'm here. Unless I'm a suspect— far-fetched considering how long those bones must've been there...."

"Slow down, Powell. This got the Rompin' Heebie Jeebies going full blast, didn't it?" My head snapped around and he waved me down exclaiming: "Don't give me that look. Of course I know about it. I'm only a Louisville city cop, but I got friends in the bureau and I like to know who I'm dealin' with. Saint Dallas Powell of the hard head and soft heart. Now shuddup an' siddown, you're makin' a scene."

I examined Ray Levitz in a new light. His bumpkinish manner made it easy to underestimate him. Quite on purpose, I imagine. Abruptly, he slid behind a table that commanded a clear view of the investigation across the way, grabbed a laminated menu and announced: "They got a turkey soup and sandwich combo here that's deadly at thirty paces."

Okay. Changing subjects was fine by me. I said: "Sounds good, you buyin'?"

A grin flashed over the top of the menu, then Levitz turned toward the counter, pointed at the "Today's Specials" board and held up two fingers. Guess he was. He turned back to me and said: "Blame the Burgess Insurance Corporation for you bein' here. When they found out the site of their new corporate headquarters had become a crime scene, they went ballistic. Started demanding an independent observer to make sure the delay didn't put construction too far behind schedule. Right away, I thought of you. Your background and experience make you a shoo-in." He paused for effect. "Unless Steadfast Investigations and Security Inc.'s tight-packed schedule won't permit it?"

I glared. Obviously he knew as well as I did Steadfast hadn't had so much as a divorce case in three weeks. Good thing the food came just then or I might've gone a little ballistic myself. Waiting for the server to do her thing, then swish her way back to the kitchen gave me time to cool my response to: "If you're finished demonstrating your investigative prowess, maybe you'd like to tell me what we're working with. You referred to the remains as 'her' earlier?"

Levitz nodded and mumbled around a mouthful of sandwich: "Aside from the shreds of one of those fancy corset-things the lab guys already bagged up, the Coroner gave me a quick take. Female, mid twenties to mid thirties. No readily apparent cause of death, but that'll change soon as they get her the rest of the way dug out. The body was found when they were breakin' up the cement floor of the old coffee-house. Lucky the demolition crew were using jackhammers; if it had been bulldozers, there probably wouldn't be much crime scene left. Been in the ground at least ten years—I'm wagering more like eighty, myself. Get a load of the pretty that was pinned to the corset." With that pronouncement, he tossed me a stack of instant Polaroids of the crime scene.

I examined the pictures while I sampled the soup. The soup was as good as advertised but the photos showed both a close-up of a Victorian-looking brooch and that Levitz wasn't as all-knowing as he liked to appear. I tossed the stack back onto the table stating: "1928."

Levitz choked and clapped a hand over his mouth to catch a spray of masticated sourdough. He swallowed hard and rasped: "Jee-zuz, Powell. You know the date of her death just by looking at a *pin*? What kind of voodoo do they teach you guys at Quantico?"

It was my turn to smile as I returned: "Not her date of death, she hasn't been dead near that long. 1928 is the company that made the brooch." My FBI training had nothing to do with the knowledge, either; I'd dated a jewelry buyer for a chain of department stores and learned more about fashion trends than I ever wanted to. The astonishment on Levitz' face almost made that three-month rollercoaster ride worthwhile. Almost.

☠ ☠ ☠ ☠ ☠ ☠ ☠

When my apartment doorbell rang one evening later that week, I thought it was the delivery kid from the Pizza King down the street. Instead it was Levitz with a thick manila envelope under his arm. I was proud of my restraint as I stepped back to let him in and said: "Levitz you sonuvabitch! You've been ducking my calls."

Levitz laughed: "Good to see you, too, Powell. Nice digs. Ya gonna ask me to sit down or just snarl at me from the doorway?"

"I might ask you to take a header off the fire escape. You set me up, Levitz, you told Dan Ellington at Burgess I was your choice for the company's police liaison then you leave me flapping in the wind with no information and Ellington calling me twice a day for the last four days."

"Shoulda come down to the station."

"I did. You'd 'just stepped out'— three days in a row. Right."

Levitz flumphed onto the couch anyway. "Musta been Sergeant Searcy, he never knows what's goin' on."

Levitz must have a guardian angel because the kid with the pizza came through the still-open door behind me: "Eighteen sixty, Mr. Powell." He looked down at the floor and grinned. "Hey, Hoover, how's it goin'?"

Hoover's my cat. Well sort of my cat— he came with the apartment. He's either a gray Persian mix or a long-haired gray tabby who's been chasing parked cars and caught one. I scowled at the cat and asked: "Where have you been all day? It's an epidemic. Ignore Dallas, then show up on his doorstep when dinner comes."

Yep, he ignored me. Currently, he was making nice with the pizza kid. I fished out a twenty and handed it to the kid, who brightened: "Gee, thanks Mr. Powell." Then disappeared down the stairs. He could have at least waited for me to tell him to keep the change.

I kicked the door closed and busied myself with paper plates. Okay, I hate doing dishes. Sue me. "You better be here for more than mooching pizza, Ray."

"Hey, Powell, I'm wounded. You'd begrudge a smidge of pizza to the bearer of an eye-popping forensics report?"

Smidge. In his whole life, Levitz never settled for a smidge of anything.

I made a noncommittal noise and poured kitty crunchies onto a paper plate, then yanked off a chunk of cheese and sausage and dropped it on top of the crunchies. As I put it on the floor in front of Hoover, Levitz snorted: "Powell, you're a loon. You name your cat after J. Edgar and you feed him pizza?"

I piled pizza on two other paper plates and plunked one plate and a roll of paper towels on the coffee table near Levitz. I dug into my pizza saying: "He got his name partly because of his face, but mostly because of how he vacuums up food— and yes, I give him pizza. It's a lot easier than battling him for every bite I take."

Levitz nodded as if it all made perfect sense to him and we munched in silence for a couple minutes. When I'd taken the edge off my hunger, I motioned toward the manila envelope and said: "Okay, you've had your pizza, now pop my eyes."

Levitz looked smug: "Bet I can surprise you this time— it's a guy."

He did. I began: "But the Coroner said...."

"That was before they got her— *him* dug out. Once the Coroner saw the pelvis free of the dirt, she about had a fit. Said something about being fooled by the lacies and a gracile bone structure. Bet I don't have to tell you that changed our ID search criteria a little."

"Good thing the skeleton was complete, we could have been spinning our wheels in the wrong direction for a long time to come. You got a name yet?"

"Yeah. That's where *I* get a surprise: Our vic is none other than Jess Wynan."

"You say that like I should recognize the name."

"I keep forgetting you're not from around here. The Wynans been in building for almost as long as Louisville's been here. Jess' daddy built the business into one of the biggest contracting concerns around. When daddy keeled over on the back nine with a coronary, he left Jess a bundle along with control of the family business. Jess wanted to be a big shot and started throwing money around. Got into politics in a small way and got heavy into the renovation of the downtown area for the Bicentennial doings. That's where we have our connection with the Hammonds."

"Ah, now this name I know. Weren't they the owners of the whole block Burgess bought and the coffeehouse in particular?"

"Bingo. Sherm and Delia Hammond. Real savory characters and a marriage made in hell. Right around the mid-Seventies, Sherm and Delia decided they wanted to clean up their act— sort of. They got into the "Beautify Bicentennial Louisville" bit same time as Jess. Looks like it was a Wynan grant helped them give the old pile a face-lift right around the time Jess disappeared.

"We also got a cause of death— several powerful blows to the

back of the head with a hammer. Looks like the killer was real P.O.ed at ol' Jess. One whack woulda done the job, but the Coroner figures more like five. Plus, there's blond and brown hairs caught in the wound as well as nylon mesh fibers. The brown hairs match the hair found in the grave; we figger he was wearin' a wig when he got clobbered. Fits with the lacy long-johns."

"It all fits, why do I think you don't like it?"

"I dunno. Maybe because this guy never struck me as the queer type— I mean, he was one of the town's biggest playboys. Always had a pretty woman on his arm. Hard to think of this guy prancing around in a wig and corset."

I smirked: "Hey, they claim J. Edgar himself went in drag."

It was Levitz' turn to glare. He opened his mouth to retort, but instead bellowed and dived for the floor. I was startled until Hoover (the cat, not the other guy) shot from under the coffee table and vanished out the catflap with the last of Levitz' pizza in his teeth.

☠ ☠ ☠ ☠ ☠ ☠

Turns out Levitz came to my place so I could go with him to question Delia Hammond; Sherm was ten years dead and Delia didn't look to be far behind. She was out at the Whispering Oaks Convalescent Home in the terminal stages of emphysema.

I'd heard Whispering Oaks was an upscale place, but that didn't half cover it. It was a stone mansion surrounded by a couple acres of manicured grounds and an eight-foot high brick wall. The only public entrance was a set of big iron gates they must've bought off a bankrupt English manor. There was probably a separate entrance for staff and other low-life, but Levitz pulled his unmarked sedan up to the main gate. It was closed, but there was one of those little intercom/closed circuit TV units set into the wall on the driver's side. Levitz punched the button and held his shield and ID up to the tiny camera. "Detective Ray Levitz from Louisville Police. You got somebody in charge out here?"

The lobby must have come from the same English manor with dark oak paneling and a huge crystal chandelier. A severe-looking woman in a no frills beige linen suit met us under the chandelier. From her expression, I gathered she'd like to have dropped the thing on us and be done with it. She said: "I'm Mrs. Le Coeur, the nursing supervisor. How may I help you?"

Levitz flipped his ID case open again. "I'm Detective Ray Levitz of Louisville Police and this is Mr. Dallas Powell representing the Burgess Insurance Corporation. We'd like to speak with a patient of yours, Mrs. Delia Hammond."

Neither ID nor introduction made a dent. "Visiting hours are from 8 a.m. to 7 p.m."

"I'm aware of that ma'am, but we need to speak to Mrs. Hammond now— it's police business."

She relented and ordered us to come to her office. I felt like a ten-year-old caught with a *Playboy* magazine in school. The impression was heightened when she sat behind a desk the size of a helipad and lifted the telephone saying: "Mrs. Hammond is under private care, you'll have to speak with her nurse, Ms. Soward. I'll have her here in a minute."

Levitz was undeterred. "Thank you for the offer, Mrs. Le Coeur, but I think we'd rather talk someplace else if you don't mind."

She minded, but she took us to a visitor area anyway. Looking around the room, I wondered if they'd simply bought a whole manor house and reconstructed it stone by stone in Louisville. I lowered myself into a chair that was probably worth more than my car and asked: "So what was wrong with Mrs. Le Coeur's office?"

Levitz looked at me like I'd sprouted a tail. "You really think the Grand Pooh-Bah would vacate to let us talk to the nurse by our lonesome? Nu uh. I know the type. She'd at least have had her ear glued to the intercom pickup." He stomped around examining the walls, stopped in front of a huge floral spray and allowed: "If there's an intercom in this room, I can't find it. Old biddy was sure P.O.ed, wasn't she? Never trust anyone like that in a room with an intercom." He took in the rest of the room and spat: "Crime don't pay, huh? Couldn't prove it by me. Damn. My Mammaw was a saint if there ever was one and the place she spent her final years wasn't as nice as this place's mop closet."

He broke off as a beautiful brunette in a nurse's uniform came to the door. Her eyes flicked nervously between us. "Are you the policemen who want to see Mrs. Hammond?"

I smiled and jerked a thumb at Levitz. "He is, I'm Dallas Powell, a Private Investigator representing the Burgess Insurance Corporation. Are you Ms. Soward?"

"Phyllis Soward." Her handshake was firm and dry. She smiled ruefully: "You're going to be really mad, but I can't let you in to see Mrs. Hammond."

Scowling, Levitz stepped forward with the ubiquitous ID out. "Detective Ray Levitz. May I ask why not?"

Ms. Soward didn't flinch but gave the big cop a cool, steady look and said: "It isn't my decision. I have standing orders not to let anyone into her room without family or doctor permission."

I stepped in: "Does she have many visitors?"

"I couldn't say. I've only been tending her for a month, but in the time I've been with her, there haven't been many."

"You're new then?"

She laughed: "Very few of Mrs. Hammond's employees are old hands. She's been here ten months and I'm nurse number eight." She went quiet and I could see indecision flash across her face, then she glanced out in the hall before continuing: "From what I understand, Delia Hammond has never had a sunny attitude and the pain she's in doesn't help an already foul temper. She heaps abuse on anyone who comes into range— she's made a point of not remembering my name, if that tells you anything."

It told me this was a lady not incredibly happy with her job. I asked: "Why do you stick it out?"

"I've never been a quitter, Mr. Powell. You know she's terminal?" At my nod, she continued: "I've tended terminal patients before and all the signs are there, it won't be long now. I can put up with the unpleasantness for a little longer. The conditions are bad, but the paycheck is good and the signing bonus I got was sweet."

I glanced at Levitz to see if he had anything to add, but he seemed content to let me do the asking. I plunged on: "Does Delia keep up on the news?"

Phyllis rolled her eyes. "I'll say! I have to read the paper to her every morning from front page to comics."

"Then she's heard about the skeleton they found at the Burgess construction site. Did she have a reaction to the news?"

"Her reaction was odd. She made me read parts of the story twice. Been quieter since. It was like— I don't know— kind of like the other shoe finally dropped? You know what I mean?"

"Yeah. I think I do."

Her face clouded as she clicked two and two together. "The paper said that was a murder. Is that what all this is about?"

"It's connected, yes."

Levitz piped up: "Gonna let us talk to Delia now?"

She shook her head. "Look, I'm not trying to be difficult, but I have my instructions from her daughter, Jessica— *Ms*. Hammond. I can't let anyone in unless she gives the okay. I don't ask why, I just cash the paycheck— the really *nice* paycheck. Believe you me, if it wasn't so nice, you'd be either eating my dust or talking to someone else.

"It's not like it would do you much good if I let you in, anyway. She's had her evening meds already and the stuff they've got her on knocks her out for at least six hours." A pause. "Seven if I'm lucky."

Levitz groused, but there wasn't much he could do about it short of getting a warrant and he didn't have near enough to do that yet. I enjoyed watching Ray squirm, grinned at Phyllis and pressed my business card into her hand. "Okay, we'll talk to Ms. Hammond, but how about you slip this to *Mrs*. Hammond when she wakes up. That's not exactly letting anyone in, right?"

She took the card with a doubtful look and I noticed she made no promises to deliver it. Instead, she pulled a small notebook and a gold pen from her pocket, wrote and ripped the page out. She handed me the page. "This is Jessica Hammond's address and phone number. I wish you luck with her. I have as little to do with her as possible— it isn't that she's the termagant her mother is, but I plain don't like her. She's dumped responsibility of her mother on me, the doctors and the staff of Whispering Oaks and makes no secret she's glad to be shed of her and finally do as she pleases. I don't know, maybe if my mother was as nasty as Delia, I'd do the same."

☠ ☠ ☠ ☠ ☠ ☠ ☠

Even though it was late, we headed over to Jessica Hammond's place. We didn't bother to call first, from the scathing looks the Nursing Su-

pervisor gave us as we left, we figured she'd called ahead. She had. When we pulled into the driveway and got out of the car, the door to the house flew open and a woman silhouetted against the interior light called: "Who the hell are you? You're not my lawyer— if you're the cops, you can just cool your heels until my legal advisor gets here."

This was bad. I had images of Levitz and me sitting in the car waiting to be chewed up one side and down the other by ravening lawyers. I was wrong. Jessica Hammond was too young and too fired-up to do the smart thing and close the door on us. She came tearing down her front steps shrilling: "How dare you disturb a dying woman at this time of night? Nothing can be that important. I'll have you know I've already lodged a complaint with your superiors!" And she hadn't even asked for ID.

Levitz went through his usual spiel, holding his shield and card toward the light spilling from the open door. I admired his tenacity; so far all his bit had accomplished was to open the gate at Whispering Oaks; this time it had an effect, but not the one he wanted. Upon hearing my name and who I represented, she turned on me: "I don't understand what problem Burgess has that involves Mother, the sale is a done deal. Mother had nothing to do with it."

Snapping his ID case closed, Levitz moved in. "Maybe you haven't heard they found the remains of a murder victim under the cement floor of the building your parents owned?"

This was old news and we were boring her already. "Of course I did. My parents used to own that whole block— they owned a lot of property in the Louisville area. So?"

Something wasn't clicking with her. "So we found somebody whose head was bashed in buried in the basement of a building your parents ran a business out of and we want to talk to your mama about it."

She exhaled an exasperated humph, then: "Lots of people ran businesses out of that building. I'd imagine most of them had access to the basement, why not go bother them? This doesn't have anything to do with us."

I asked: "It doesn't? What do you know about Jess Wynan?"

She turned toward me so that the light from the door fell across her, revealing a delicate face at odds with the shrill voice. She asked: "Who? Oh, I remember...the Wynan Old Louisville Trust. My parents had some business dealings with them. He had something to do with real estate didn't he? Oh. Was that him—I thought the papers said it was a woman's body...."

Levitz supplied: "Contracting, not real estate and yes, the remains have been identified as those of Jess Wynan who has been missing since 1975."

She shrugged: "I couldn't have known him then, I wasn't born until 1976. Look, will you get to the point? I have an early day tomorrow."

I interjected: "Dan Ellington of Burgess Insurance tells us that they've been trying to buy that property for a couple years and your mother wouldn't sell. Suddenly, you took their offer. Why was that?"

For the first time Jessica looked doubtful, but she dismissed it. She said: "My parents ran a little coffee shop down there. Mother had certain sentimental attachments to the area and didn't want to see an impersonal office building go in there. My parents gifted me the properties on my twenty-first birthday. Nothing warm and maternal on my mother's part, I assure you, it was in my father's will and my mother's way to cheat the state out of inheritance taxes."

Her answer was very flat. Cold. I stated: "And you sold it."

"They offered me a lot of money, and I don't have those sentiments."

Or many others, I'll wager. Headlights from a car pulling into the drive in back of us flooded the scene with a blinding glare. The driver got out without shutting off the engine or the lights. Jessica glanced at the newcomer approaching our little group and said loudly: "I'm afraid I'm going to have to refuse you. I can't allow you to disturb a dying old woman with questions she couldn't possibly answer."

Levitz snarled: "Okay. We'll just have to talk to a judge, then."

The newcomer was the tardy lawyer. He interjected: "You do that, mister. You'd better have a warrant before you come sniffing around Ms. Hammond or her mother again, or I'll have your badges."

The lawyer and Levitz locked horns for a few more minutes, leaving Jessica Hammond and me on the outskirts of the battle. I took the opportunity to give her a once over. She was tall, slim and expensively dressed. Her dark hair was done up in the latest style— fairly recently from the look of it. She stood in the glare of the lawyer's headlights,

lit a cigarette and settled back to enjoy the fight. I watched her revel in her newly-acquired power and found myself agreeing with Phyllis Soward's assessment of the lady.

It was extremely late by the time I got home and fell into bed.

☒ ☒ ☒ ☒ ☒ ☒

As I slipped the key into the office door the next morning, I heard the phone ringing. I fumbled the lock open and dived for the receiver before the fourth ring faded. "Steadfast Investigation and Security, Inc. This is Dallas Powell speaking."

There was a sigh of relief on the other end and a woman's voice came over the wire: "Thank God I finally got you, Mr. Powell. This is Phyllis Soward—we met last night at the Whispering Oaks Convalescent Center?"

"Yes, Ms. Soward, I remember. You sound rattled, has something happened?"

"I'll say it has. When Mrs. Hammond woke up earlier this morning I told her about your visit and gave her your card like you asked. I thought she was having another attack. She insisted I call you right away and well, your home number wasn't on the card and you aren't in the Louisville directory...."

"It wouldn't be: I live in New Albany. Does Mrs. Hammond want to see me? That might be difficult, her daughter refused to let us interview her. Even sicced an attack lawyer on us."

Phyllis laughed a little in spite of everything, then caught herself. "I don't think that'll be a problem. Delia is causing such a fuss and refusing any medications until you get here, Mrs. Le Coeur will be overjoyed to see you. She might even carry you into the room herself."

"Let me get Detective Levitz and we're on our way."

She thanked me and apologized again for calling so early before she hung up. I dialed Levitz and crossed my fingers hoping this case would last long enough I for me to get to know Phyllis better. Sgt. Searcy picked up at the police station and I said: "This is Dallas Powell for Ray Levitz, and before you tell me he isn't available, maybe you ought to tell him I got us in to see Delia Hammond right away." Worked like a charm. Levitz didn't bother to pick up, just had Searcy tell me to be ready to roll when he got to my doorstep.

☒ ☒ ☒ ☒ ☒ ☒ ☒

Phyllis was right, Mrs. Le Coeur all but welcomed us in with open arms and ushered us into Delia's room quickly. Delia Hammond was propped up in a hospital bed surrounded with starched white pillows and sheets that accented the unhealthy yellow of her skin and eyes. She glared at Mrs. Le Coeur who said: "These are the gentlemen from the police you wanted to see." Le Coeur and Phyllis beat a hasty retreat and looking on the face of the Dragon Lady herself, I wished I could go with them.

Delia didn't waste any time. She rasped: "So you found Jess. You do know it was Jess Wynan, doncha?"

Nonplussed, Levitz plopped into a chair: "If I'da known this was gonna be a confession, I'da brought a tape recorder or somethin'."

She coughed, then: "Tough, you can write it down later, you got more time than I do. Lissen up. We met Jess Wynan through the Old Louisville Trust. We got a grant to pretty up the old building our store was in. Place was a dump, but had history, so we got the money and we got to know Jess. Jess knew Louisville was growin' fast and wanted to buy into the downtown district, but on the QT. Me and Sherm had lots of connections and was wantin' to improve our own financial situation, too. So Jess made us some private loans and we was buyin' up property around Louisville, slow-like so as not to draw a lot of attention.

"Pretty soon Jess made advances t'me and I didn't say no. Do I look stupid? He was a real looker and all that Wynan money didn't hurt none. Trouble was Sherm was always having flings of his own and one night I come to the store unexpected-like and found Sherm and this blonde rollin' around in the back room. Now I mighta been foolin' around, too, but I done it discrete, y'know, away from our own place. Well, I yelled at 'em and the woman turns around and damn if it wasn't Jess in drag.

"I didn't take that real good. My face musta been a sight because Jess just laughed and laughed. Honest, I don't remember what happened after that, I just remember comin' to on th' floor with Sherm wrestlin' me for a hammer.

"We didn't know what to do. We was just gettin' legit and here this happens. We figure who's gotta know? Nobody knew our relation-ship with Jess Wynan was more than the Old Louisville stuff and if anyone knew Jess swung both ways, they wasn't gonna say it— not in '75.

"We dragged him to the basement where we was fixin' the floor, dropped him in, poured quick lime over him and covered him up. Whole place was gettin' a redo then so nobody paid any attention to cement work or anything else. When we was done, we found out his wig come off on the stairs, so we tied it to the hammer an' tossed 'em both in the river."

Levitz had been scribbling madly during her monologue. I'd sneaked a peek and almost laughed out loud when I recognized the chicken scratches on the pad as shorthand. Who'da thunk it, right? Anyway, when she paused, Ray looked up and asked: "Okay, you kept quiet about this all these years why come clean now?"

Delia snorted, then disintegrated into a coughing fit. She smacked my hand away from the nurse call button and sucked oxygen until the spasm subsided. She gasped in answer: "You found him, dincha? I'm dyin' anyway, what difference is it gonna make to me? I mean what ya gonna do— give me the death penalty? Besides, if I don't own up now, it might cause problems for the kid. She's a little bitch, but I don't want that."

Delia waved her hand petulantly. "Shoulda listened to me. I told her not to sell that parcel but does she listen? Not a bit! Didn't even bother to consult her old lady about it first. Bet this'll play hob with her high society dreams. I saw this comin' when Sherm set it up so's she'd get her money when she turned twenty-one, but he never lis-tened to me, neither. She's tryin' to be too high class for her own good— well, you seen her."

Levitz was gathering his things to leave and not knowing what else to say I replied: "Your daughter is a very beautiful woman."

Delia snorted again, although this time more successfully. She allowed: "Yeah, looks just like her daddy does Jessica."

As we left, I thought I heard her mutter: "Dresses like him, too." But I can't swear to it.

☠ ☠ ☠ ☠ ☠ ☠

Levitz stomped out of the room and for the parking lot, punctuating each footfall with a new swearword— it was an impressive vocabulary. I caught up with him at the car. He was leaning against the trunk looking out over the sunset-stained panorama. He said: "I remember when Jess Wynan turned up missing. It was one of the first cases I worked. I remember at the time I was surprised at how no one seemed all that bent out of shape he was gone and not all that anxious to get him back. Wonder how many of 'em suspected what really happened?"

"You gonna ask them?"

He dug out the keys and spat: "Hell no! I think I'm just gonna concentrate on ducking when this goes public."

Scenes From a Murder
by Dirk Griffin

iii

following beauty
his blue eyes quiet
his youth shining
his smile shy
his manner gentle

at the table
absorbed in one another
place and time trivial
speaking a language of oneness
conversations of
dancing words
dancing melodies
dancing bodies
of lifetimes together

blond hair falls over his eyes
enshrouding them with darkness
he is silent
she touches him
he looks away
and back to her

her words return his smile
brushing away darkness

The Blue Heron
by Jeannine Baumgartle

The day was definitely worth talking about: cream-colored circles of cloud pasted on a turquoise sky, bare tree branches fencing their view as they walked (and talked) like usual. Water from the hills leaked across the road in black streaks; the noon sun, incredibly sweet for the middle of March, filled the air with warm humidity. It was all so pleasant. Sue charitably credited it to El Niño, even after the winter it had given them. Lisa plodded along beside her, smiling, determined to get full benefit out of her lunch-hour walk.

Sue was the only employee in the small-town Post Office, and so was obliged— required by government bureaucracy as well—to shut down at noon every day in order to have lunch. Since she'd rather walk than eat, here they were, all but jogging down the country road, following the creek. Two miles was all they had time (or energy) for, both of them almost 50.

Again they remarked on the news the night before, how some guy had got into a high-speed chase over a few traffic violations, and ended up shooting one of the policemen.

"His whole life, down the tubes for nuthin'," Sue commented, wagging her head over the stupidity of it.

"Um," Lisa agreed. "His family, his job— pretty expensive panic attack— Not to mention the poor policeman's family. Guy like that; wonder if they'll go with a psychiatric evaluation."

"Haven't caught him yet," Sue puffed, tennies plopping along, arms pumping to get the full range of cardiovascular stimulation.

"Well, I just heard the first part," Lisa pardoned herself. "Had to take off. Book club meeting last night at the coffee house."

"So, read any good books lately?"

"Yeah; ate some good cheesecake, too. Cheesecake and sarsaparilla. That's why I gotta do this!" She hustled extra hard to exaggerate her point and they both laughed.

The winding hill at the far end of their walk was the hardest part. The county hadn't got to this road for a while and the edges were beginning to crumble. They had to walk near the center and listen for cars. No point in fixing it for a while, though, with all the new construction going on. Little house after little house was being planted along the steep incline with just barely enough driveway to get the owners off the road.

The hazardous curve was always on their minds as Lisa and Sue plodded toward the one-mile marker, the telephone pole with yellow cables securing it to the rocky hillside. At the top, they stood a minute, panting, knees still picking themselves up to accommodate the pumping blood, then they gave themselves to gravity, accelerating into a downhill pace.

Last week the roadside trash had finally gotten to them and they'd taken garbage bags along and started collecting on the downhill trek. Mostly fast food wrappers, that and beer bottles and cans. Very few of the brown bottles were broken, and they seemed to have been dumped in groups, as though whoever did it finished the entire carton before hurling the empties out the window.

They knew most of the people who traveled this road. They were neighbors and postal patrons who swerved way out for them and smiled and waved, and kept neat yards. Then there were the delivery trucks and pickups carrying supplies to the new construction. The work crews came and went but they probably brought their lunches. No fast food places around here. Sue speculated that it was the "shortcut" people, cutting through the country from the Interstate to Highway 335, who were tossing stuff out.

It took two days' walk to complete the cleanup, with Lisa going back later in the car to pick up the bags they'd filled. Then they had their country scenery to enjoy again in all the lovely variations of the seasons. Now all they had to do was not get run over—

—Whew! They stepped out of the damp weeds and brushed themselves off.

"Did you happen to catch that license number?" Underneath Sue's laid-back inquiry was a tone of shaky outrage.

"Just a zip of teal." Lisa slid her hands past each other to create friction, to illustrate how fast it had disappeared.

☒ ☒ ☒ ☒ ☒ ☒ ☒

The morning news carried over the speed-chase story, Lisa discovered. She sifted through the parts she already knew, at the same time pulling on her socks and shoes and calling out patiently "in your backpack" and "get your Dad a towel out of the dryer" and "your watch? Check the upstairs bathroom." The incident was attributed to road-rage, the reporter was saying. The driver of the car had apparently sat in traffic as long as he could stand it, then taken off the wrong way up an exit ramp, and was spotted by police as he attempted to cross a median to go the other way. He'd stopped and hurled a bottle at the police car as it rocked and rolled onto the inverted median, then as quickly, pulled out a gun, fired, and took off.

The policeman's partner had radioed in their position, and a chase followed. The car was a teal Ford Mustang, but they were unable to get the license number. They traced him to Louisville, but it was hard to do a high-speed chase in the morning commute. —Hard to do a morning commute in a morning commute, Lisa thought, glad all over again that she didn't have to and could just take care of her family and write. — The police picked up the bottle the guy had thrown, a sarsaparilla bottle, and were holding it as evidence, hoping to get fingerprints.

☒ ☒ ☒ ☒ ☒ ☒ ☒

Her computer locked up at a reasonable time for once, Lisa thought. It was almost noon, and time to walk.

Sue closed the P.O. and they set out, this time under cloudy skies. It was still warm though, would probably rain tonight. Across the tracks and the bridge over the little creek. The water gurgled happily beneath them, and a damp breeze pushed through the trees.

Maybe they were talking too loudly, because huge blue and white wings flapped and their refugee waterfowl of some kind coasted away from them along the creek bed, his wing span almost too wide for the overhanging trees. Been there a couple of months now, either recuperating or lost. "That blue heron," Sue called it, whether it was one or not.

Lots of things took refuge in these hills. Like deer, hunted to the verge of town, and Mo-ped riders, and the folk who moved out this way wanting a little piece of country all their own. Not much left of retreats though, wings or no wings. Halfway up the hill they encountered broken glass and shook their heads at it. Their beautiful countryside. Lisa nudged the pieces of brown bottle off the road with her shoe, stopped suddenly to retrieve one of the shards that caught her attention.

"Look at this." She showed Sue the raised pattern of swinging doors and a man wearing a cowboy hat walking through them. "Sarsaparilla." A thought occurred to her. "What time is it?"

Sue looked slightly confused but obliged her with "12:20. Why?"

Lisa took her arm and hauled her off the roadway. They stood listening for a few seconds, apparently for nothing. So much for my theory, Lisa thought. Probably ought to take my web address off the Columbo fan page. She stepped toward the gravel edge of the road, heard Sue hiss, and was abruptly yanked backward. The wuff of a car draft nearly pulled them under. A glimpse of teal.

"Did you see that?"

"Yup. Like the back end of a June bug.

☠ ☠ ☠ ☠ ☠ ☠ ☠

It turned out to be pretty the next day. At noon, Sue and Lisa stepping-stoned their way across the middle of the small creek and hiked directly up the hillside to "the Eagle's nest," a lump of limestone jutting out like a promontory for looking over the valley. They couldn't see the beginning or end of their walk from here, just the middle, which was just as well. They probably shouldn't be here anyway, since they'd turned informant with what little information they had, and the authorities had decided to follow up on the lead, since it was the only one they had to go on.

A couple of state troopers were down by the bridge, blocking it off. Local police waited hidden in the Jeffery's driveway, just up the hill, and a plainclothes guy sat at the Y where the little gravel road branched off before the hill.

Sure enough, at about 12:20, a whoosh broke past them. They watched with interest as a wild-eyed fellow backed into view, searching in vain for a place to turn around, as the unmarked car and the county one slowly closed on him from behind. He didn't even bother to fight this time, with all the guns trained on him, but got out and raised his hands in the air and waited to be frisked and handcuffed.

Sue pressed the button on her disposable camera. So. One to hang beside her photographs of the creek and the deer and the blue heron.

Loose Money and Change
by Elizabeth J. Gross

Robert Stiner took the heavy brown suitcase from his Jaguar. Making quite sure the car doors were locked, nervously looking over his shoulder, he briskly walked to the Cuppa Joe Coffee House.

After his eyes adjusted to the dim light, he spotted a booth by a front window, went to it and sat down. He could see his car from there. The neighborhood was bad; he was afraid his car would be stolen and today, of all days, the automobile was important.

Placing the suitcase between him and the wall, he scanned the room. Six loud-mouths sat at two tables pulled together. A short bald-headed man worked behind the counter and a younger hippie-type guy with a ponytail and an earring carried a tray of coffee and sandwiches to the unruly group.

Robert glanced out the window— his car was still there. He looked at his watch: three o'clock— forty-five minutes to go.

Joe Cuppa was making two cups of cappuccino when the distinguished man came in the coffeehouse. "Class for the joint," he muttered. He set two coffees on the tray with the sandwiches, turned up his hearing aid, went over to wait on the customer. "Afternoon."

The man jumped. He had been intently watching a ragged boy taking something out of a garbage can.

"Welcome to Cuppa Joe's. I'm Joe Cuppa— what can I get for you? We have sandwiches, coffee, tea and soft drinks. Do you need a menu?" He pulled one from between the napkin holder, shakers and placed it in front of the man.

"No! No!" Robert waved his hand. "Just coffee— really HOT coffee."

"Okay," Joe said putting back the menu. "Coming right up."

☠ ☠ ☠ ☠ ☠ ☠ ☠

Tony Smith hated his job— he hated any job for that matter. Picking up the tray with the coffee and sandwiches, he started toward the table with the loud-mouths. He particularly disliked this bunch. They came in every day, sat at the same place, hooted and hollered. He had worked here nearly two weeks, which was about his normal time, and was ready to move on. He thought he would liked to have waited on the dude with the suitcase. That might have been interesting, and this could be THE BIG BREAK he had been waiting for.

"Shit!" he muttered when Joe went over. "Probably the old turd tips real good, too!"

☠ ☠ ☠ ☠ ☠ ☠ ☠

Darrell Collins slowly drove his old blue Ford by the Cuppa Joe. There was the Jaguar parked right in front. He grinned. He had been tailing Robert Stiner all day and now saw the old man carry a brown suitcase inside the coffee shop. "He's killing a little time," Darrell muttered. He turned left at the corner, went down the street to some warehouses by the river, pulled between two of the brick buildings and shut off the motor. He turned the rearview mirror around, studied himself, took a comb from his pocket, smoothed his dark brown hair. Satisfied, he flipped the mirror back, put away his comb and got out of the car.

He opened a side door, climbed a flight of stairs, pushed open another door, came out on the roof of the warehouse. He could see really well from there. "Catbird's seat," he snickered. He could see the drop-off point pretty well too, that being the small space between two buildings. Pulling up a packing crate, dusting it off, he settled down to wait for Stiner.

☠ ☠ ☠ ☠ ☠ ☠ ☠

Joe set the coffee down in front of his customer. "Thank you," Robert Stiner said, standing up. He had the suitcase in his hand. "I'm sorry— you see, there's a young boy at my car and I must..." he keeled over, grabbing the corner of the table cloth, taking the coffee cup, salt, pepper shakers, napkin holder, menu and a little box holding sugar packets to the ground with him. The shakers rolled clackety-clackety across the floor; the coffee ran to the sugar packets and puddled around them. He landed on the suitcase— breaking it open. His legs twitched then he lay still, mouth gaping and sightless eyes staring at the ceiling.

"What? Well, good God!" Joe knelt, stuck two fingers against Stiner's neck— no pulse. Jerking the tie out of its loop, grabbing the shirt with both hands, he ripped it open. The buttons hit the floor and side of the booth. Two rolled across the room and smacked the counter. They wobbled around, lay flat on the floor. Joe started CPR, "One...two...three..."

At the sound of the cup, saucer, and shakers hitting the floor, the loud-mouthed chatter stopped. A girl screamed and everyone stood up— the better to see. Tony went over to the suitcase. Money was scattered everywhere. "Whee-yoo! That damn suitcase has money in it! A freakin' ton of it!" He stooped, grabbed a handful of the money, stuffed it down his shirt.

"Tony!" Joe said between breaths. "Call 9-1-1!" He again blew in Stiner's mouth, keeping count, "One...two...."

"Gawd!" Tony said. "Gawd, Gawd, Gawd!" He shoved more money in his bulging shirt. The others had come over and were stuffing money wherever they could— in pockets, shirts, down blue jeans.

"Look at this, man!" one guy said.

"That's money!" a girl said, cashing in on the situation.

"Nooooo shit, man! A lot of it too!"

"Call 9-1-1!" Joe shouted. "This man needs help! He'll have a good chance if you do!" He started the count again as he pushed Stiner's chest.

Tony ran behind the counter, grabbed a .357 Magnum from a shelf under the cash register, sped to the front door and locked it. He loped over to the telephone and jerked the cord out of the wall.

"Ain't nobody," he screamed. "Ain't NOBODY calling no freakin' 9-1-1! Ain't nobody doing diddly-shit 'ceptin' gettin' away from the money and gettin' back against that wall!" He jerked the gun toward the back of the café.

"Hey, you!" he pointed to a girl. "Come over here! Get in there and lock that back door!" Whimpering, she reluctantly came forward.

"Don't shoot! Don't shoot!" she whined, her hands held out, palms towards Tony. "I'll do it— just don't shoooot meee!"

Tony stood in the doorway, his back against the jam so he could see the girl, the back door and the others in the front room.

"Shut up!" he yelled. "If you all don't shut the shit up, I'll kill you! Got that? Lock that door!" he told the girl. "And get back in here!" She locked the door, came back, still whimpering and trembling.

"Joe! Joe! Answer me, damn it! I'm talking to you!" yelled Tony. "Get away from that stiff!" He motioned Joe away with his gun. "He's dead— dead enough anyhow!" Joe kept up the CPR rhythm. Tony loped over, put the gun to Joe's head, cocked it. "I'll blow your freakin' brains out man!" He kicked Joe in the side, knocking him off Stiner.

☒ ☒ ☒ ☒ ☒ ☒

Joe hit the floor and rolled over. He wrapped his arms around his body and held his side. He saw Tony's fly was open, the tail of his red shirt poked out and a trail of toilet paper stuck to the bottom of his shoe. A puckered lipstick blot blew Passion Pink kisses when he walked. In spite of his sore ribs, Joe laughed.

"The trouble with you, Joe, is, " Tony said standing over him, "you ain't got no freakin' sense."

☒ ☒ ☒ ☒ ☒ ☒

Twelve year old Jason Renfrow had been going through a trash can in the parking lot of the Cuppa Joe. He saw the fussed— up man in his fancy green car stop in front of the coffeehouse. The youth hitched up his ragged, filthy pants, stepped out on the sidewalk, watched the man go inside. He wondered what was so all-fired important in that suit-case that the sissified old fart would take the thing inside with him. Weren't no atty-tay-shay, he thought. Just a shitty-colored ol' suitcase.

Going around to the back of the Cuppa Joe, he pushed up a partly opened window— which he had done countless times before. Hold-ing to the windowsill, he climbed up, over and dropped with a plop on to the storeroom floor. Squatting and listening, he made sure no one was there; only then did he start to move.

He sneaked first into the little kitchen, opened the refrigerator, rammed his filthy index finger into a bowl of ham salad. He scooped up a gob, stuck it in his mouth, sucked it off his finger. Pushing his whole hand down, he brought up a handful, crammed it in his mouth, ran his tongue around on his hand and up his wrist. Some had dropped on his shirt— he pulled it up, licked it off.

The boy went over to the stove, lifted the lid off a big, bubbling pot of vegetable soup, spit in it, watched the white foamy stuff float around on top. When it had all blended away with the soup, he went over to the store room door— just in time to see the old geezer fall. Jason immediately squatted down and through the table legs, saw the suitcase break open, spilling the money on the floor.

☠ ☠ ☠ ☠ ☠ ☠ ☠

Darrell looked at his watch: four-ten— no one had come. He stood up, brushed his pants off, buttoned his jacket, eased over to the other side of the warehouse. He peered over the ledge and could see all the way out to the road— no one was in sight. Creeping all around the roof edge, looking down, he could see he was the only one around. Lifting his binoculars from his neck, he panned the area. A wind picked up, blew debris around on the ground, caught a newspaper sheet, sent it cart wheeling down the street. He could make out part of the headline FBI CLOSES... taking that as an omen, he went back across the roof, opened the door, went down and out to his car.

☠ ☠ ☠ ☠ ☠ ☠ ☠

"You! Yes! You, Asshole! Get over here and cram that dough back in that suitcase!" Tony emptied his own shirt-horde of cash onto the pile of money. A skinny young man in jeans began stuffing the bills back in the bag. Joe Cuppa sat against the wall, holding his side. He was worried about the stranger, fascinated by Tony and wondered if any ribs were broken.

"Be-cause," Tony said, "I'm such a nice guy, I'm letting all you freakin' losers keep the money you poked in your pockets." He grinned. "Close and lock that suitcase and scoot it on over here! Goody, now get back over with the others— NO! Wait! Get over there and get them keys outta that dude's pocket. I'm a takin' his dough and his fancy ride! Lay 'em on the table— fine! Now..." he waved the gun toward a wall "get in the little restroom! Jack-o," he pointed to a young man in a T-shirt that stated I'M HERE WITH DUMMY, "get over there and help Joe get up so's he can experience this little pleasure with you. Now," he said looking at their T-shirts, "where's Dummy?

He spotted her and motioned her over. "Okay, Dumb and Dumber, both you can help o' Joe in." The terrified couple pulled Joe up and led him to the small lavatory.

"Get in! Move it over— let 'em in! There!" Tony said pushing the last one in. "Cozy ain't it?" He grinned. "Now, don't you all do nuttin' I wouldn't do, you hear?" He slammed the door.

He went behind the counter, rummaged around, found the long piece of rope he was looking for. He made a knot, slipped it over the lavatory's doorknob, tied the other end around the leg of a barstool bolted to the floor.

Jason watched from the edge of the kitchen door. The guy snapped the suitcase shut and scooted it over to Tony. While Tony rummaged behind the counter for the rope, the boy sprang across the room, carried, half-dragged the suitcase across the floor back to the kitchen. All the hollering and banging from the restroom covered up any noise he made.

"SHUT THE SHIT UP!" Tony shouted, raising his head over the counter just as Jason disappeared into the kitchen.

☠ ☠ ☠ ☠ ☠ ☠

Darrell circled the block. The old man's Jaguar was still in front of the coffeehouse. "Somethin's up," He muttered, then turned left again at the corner, backed up, headed back toward the Cuppa Joe. He slipped in between two cars, turned the key off. He flipped the rear-view mirror around, smoothed his hair, pushed the mirror back, and prepared to wait.

He waited only a couple minutes, when he spied a ragged, dirty kid hauling a brown suitcase down the street. He recognized it as the one the old man had carried into the coffeehouse. The boy dragged awhile, carried awhile, trying to hurry, and disappeared around a corner.

Before Darrell could pull from his parking space, a man ran out the Cuppa Joe's door, darted one way, then the other. "That pony-tailed hippie's actin' real crazy," Darrell muttered.

☠ ☠ ☠ ☠ ☠ ☠

Tony couldn't believe his eyes! The suitcase had disappeared! "Where'd it go? Freakin' grew legs and walked off!" he muttered. He checked the storeroom— no place left unturned. "I'm freakin' going nuts, or," he said "somebody else was here!" The front door had been locked (he remembered he had locked it) when he just went outside. He ran to the back door—the bolt was on. He stopped! Realization dawned on him— THE STOREROOM WINDOW HAD BEEN OPEN! He galloped to the storeroom— the windowsill had scrape marks! He leaned out and saw where someone had scuffed up the dirt on the ground. SOMEONE HAD DRAGGED SOMETHING DOWN THE ALLEY!

Chewing the skin around his fingernails trying to decide what to do, an idea hit him. He went to the lavatory door, and spoke to it: "I'm a lettin' you out. Don't nobody try nuttin', you hear? Now, once I untie the rope on the door knob and I say so, you all come on out, one at a time— no funny stuff, got it?"

☠ ☠ ☠ ☠ ☠ ☠ ☠

Martin Bostock and Fred Keller sat with Lucy Stiner around the table in a one room cabin in the woods. They were eyeing the clock. It was nearly six o'clock, and Darrell wasn't back yet.

"Sumpin's wrong, I tell you! He shudda been back by now!"

"Aw, for crapola's sake, Martin," the short fat man said, "To you everbody's up to sumpin'. You ain't got no trust for nobody!"

"Listen, I ain't got where I'm at today by trustin' nobody!"

"And just where might that be? I ask. You're in a little shitty cabin in the big old woods sittin' at a table with me and Lucy Stiner a waitin' for Darrell Collins TO COME BACK AND TELL US IF HER OLD MAN," Fred yelled, pointing at Lucy "BROUGHT THE DOUGH OR NOT!" He narrowed his eyes at Martin. "I'd say you were pretty well ee-stab-lished in the world, ain't you?" Martin opened his mouth to say something then snapped it shut.

"Anyways," Fred continued, "Ford Motor Company comes a barreling outta there like a bat outta hell at three o'clock. He's in that mess somewheres. If'n he ain't here in an hour, THEN we start worrin'."

"Well," the big man said, "All I'm a sayin' is, if'n he knows what's good for him, he better NOT be tryin' nuttin'." Martin lit a Marlboro, clanked shut his lighter, went to the window. He peered down the dirt road that disappeared into some pine trees.

"The bastard better not double cross us!" he muttered, drawing a long drag on his cigarette. "He'll sure as hell be sorry!"

Fred, with his eyes still on the clock, screwed up his face in a thoughtful way and drummed his fingers on the table.

"Yeah, he'll sure as hell be sorry!" repeated Martin.

☠ ☠ ☠ ☠ ☠ ☠ ☠

Darrell drove slowly, carefully keeping the boy and the suitcase in sight. After three blocks, the youngster went into a two-story brick house. There was a CONDEMNED sign on the door. Parking a half block down, Darrell got out of the car, straightened his sports jacket, adjusted his tie. He went up to the building, eased the door open, slipped inside, listened. Placing his feet gingerly on each step, he slowly went up.

At the top, a board creaked— he froze. No one came. A scuffling noise, the word "Shit" came from a room to his right. Easing to the door, looking in, he saw the boy slide the suitcase into a hole in the wall. Casing the room, seeing only the youngster, Darrell said, "Ain't no use in putting that suitcase too far in that hole, boy, you'll just hafta drag it back out again." The kid jumped, turned around, saw the man by the door.

"Stay away from that window, you little shit, or," Darrell pulled a gun from a holster under his jacket, "I'll shoot you deadern a door nail." He cocked the gun. "Get back there!" he waved the gun toward the hole. "And get that suitcase outen that hole, there. NOW! You dirty little turd!" The boy reached back in the hole and dragged the suitcase out.

"Over here! Bring it over here!" Darrell said pointing the gun at the floor. The kid dragged the suitcase over and spit on the man's shiny white loafers. Darrell hit the youngster across the face, splitting his lip, knocking him to the floor.

☠ ☠ ☠ ☠ ☠ ☠ ☠

"All right!" Tony said. "Empty your pockets. Gimmee all your money, includin' what you stuffed in your clothes. Okay, so I'm an Indian Giver," he snickered, "so sue me." One by one each of the hostages emptied their pockets and wallets, laid the money on a table. He scooped it up, stuffed it down his shirt.

"Now, get back in the toilet!" He pushed two people to speed them up. After he closed the lavatory door, he again tied the rope around the doorknob and the stool. He punched NO SALE on the cash register, pocketed the cash. Sticking his gun in his waistband, he went over to Stiner, took his money and credit cards. He stuck the man's diamond ring on his pinkie— he thought it looked impressive. He went to the lavatory, knocked, said, "Well, good-bye Joe, me gotta go— catch you turkeys later now, you hear?" trotted out the door, got in Stiner's green Jaguar and drove away.

☠ ☠ ☠ ☠ ☠ ☠ ☠

It was a little past six o'clock when Darrell got to the cabin.

"WHERE IN THE HELL'VE YOU BEEN?" Martin yelled. "Where's the damn money?" he demanded when he saw Darrell was empty handed.

"He never showed up," Darrell said looking in a dresser mirror, smoothing his hair.

"WHAT THE SHIT YOU MEAN HE NEVER SHOWED UP?" Martin screeched.

"Just what I said. He never came. He wasn't there. He didn't show. No Bob Stiner. No payola. How much clearer you want it?"

"Don't get smart with me, you snot-nosed kid! We shoulda' known better than to give a man-sized job to a damn baby!" He yanked Darrell around, grabbed his jacket, wadding it up. "You can't do a damn thing right! Hell, I oughta kill you here and now!" He lifted Darrell up on tiptoes, narrowed his eyes at him and growled "You better not be tryin' to pull sumpin' over on us, 'cause if you are, you'll sure as blazes be sorry!"

"Hey! Hey!" Fred said going over to Martin. "We don't need no more trouble, man!" Turning to Darrell he told him, "Like he said, you better not be up to nuttin', and if you're lyin', I just might beat the shit outta you, myself!"

"I waited at the drop-off until five-thirty. Nobody never showed up," Darrell said, smoothing his crumpled jacket. "I drove straight here— that's all there is to tell you. I don't know nothin' else!" He and Martin glared at each other.

"Commere, Lucy," Fred said, motioning to the petite blonde. She came over and he went on to say, "What you think happened to your old man? Why didn't he bring the dough?"

"I don't know," she said, truly puzzled, "I sure thought he would. Maybe he smelled a rat, I don't know."

"Hey! wait a minute!" Martin said turning up the volume on the television. "Listen to this!"

"...of a heart attack," a pretty blonde anchor woman was saying. "We'll give you a recap: the man who died of an apparent heart attack during the robbery in a west end coffee house was Mr. Robert Stiner, CEO of Stiner Enterprises. Joe Cuppa, owner of the Cuppa Joe Coffee House, tried in vain to revive him. Stiner was pronounced dead on arrival at University Hospital. He was a very prominent figure in the state. He has served on the City Council, Board of Trustees at the University Hospital, was greatly responsible for the re-election of several senators, mayors, and most recently, he, himself was in a very heated race for governor. He is survived by his wife, the former Eileen Phillips, daughter of the late Senator John Phillips. He also has one child, Lucy. We offer our deepest sympathies to his family."

The male anchor took over: "At the White House today..." Fred pushed the OFF button; the screen went blank.

"Well," he said, "I guess that answers a lotta questions."

"Now what'll we do?" whined Martin.

"Gimme time to think, Jughead! Commere, Lucy! Have any idea where that dough got to? He musta had it, since he was that close!"

"I have no idea! I guess he had it there in that coffeehouse with him. Either it's in his car— or the police have it...maybe the robber stole it!"

"Now, what'll we do?" Martin whined again. "It's all for nuttin'!"

"Aw, simmer down!" said Fred. "Darrell, where's the old shit's car? Did you see it?"

Darrell thought a minute. "No," he lied.

Martin grabbed Lucy up against him, twisting her arm behind her. "If'n you're tryin' sumpin', I'll kill you!" He gave her arm an upward jerk— she yelled.

"Hey, stop that shit!" Darrell thumped Martin on his arm. "Let her go!" He glared at Martin.

"Who're you to tell me what to do, you little punk?" He let Lucy go, went for Darrell. Fred elbowed between them.

"Stop it! Quit your eternal fightin'! Ain't nobody tryin' nuttin'! It happened! The old shit died! UP AND DIED!" He pushed Martin back. "Sit down, you big dummy. Gimme time to think! Now, Lucy," he turned toward her, "What about the will? You oughta be gettin' pretty rich— how much, you reckon?"

"Not a dime!" she said, rubbing her arm, "What I get is in a trust fund. I'll get about twenty thousand a year— no more! It'll all go to Eileen."

"Your step-ma. Can we put a bite on her for ransom?"

"Fat chance!" snorted Lucy. "She wouldn't give a cent to save my life— she'd laugh and tell you to go to hell!"

"Darrell, think you might nose around and try to find out where that dough got to?"

"I could, but I suspect I won't turn up nuttin'."

"Well, ask around anyways— see what you can turn up. Nuttin' for you, Lucy , but to go play the lovin' daughter right now. Martin, me and you gotta be gone awhile. We'll all meet back here by Thursday."

☠ ☠ ☠ ☠ ☠ ☠ ☠

Two days later, on Wednesday afternoon, Darrell Collins drove his brand new red Corvette down Main Street, turned right at the corner of Rowan, then left again on Market. Just ahead was his destination— the Cuppa Joe Coffee House. He parked the car, pulled the rearview mirror around, slicked back his hair, flipped the glass back. Getting out, he straightened his tie with the big fish on it and buttoned his sports jacket. He ran the front of his shoes up the back of his creased slacks, giving them a big shine. Satisfied, he went in the coffeehouse. It was crowded inside— lunch time! Looking around, he spotted her. He made his way to the booth in the corner, sat down. Lucy Stiner looked up.

"Did anyone see you?"

"Nah! It's okay."

"Good", she sighed.

☠ ☠ ☠ ☠ ☠ ☠ ☠

Joe Cuppa was behind the counter making a cappuccino. He looked up as Darrell came in. He didn't know why, but instinct told him to watch the man. Joe had his hearing aid turned off, as he usually did when a lot of people were there— the noise got on his nerves. The man sat down with the pretty blonde woman in the corner booth. Joe did what he did really well— he read lips. He saw Darrell mouth "Nah! It's okay." Then, "Look, I rented an apartment over at The Meadows out on Locust Street— you know the place?" The girl nodded. "Well, here's the key." He slid something across the table. "The apartment number is twenty-seven. The suitcase is under the bed." Joe's interest picked up. "If anything happens to me, I want you to get it and GET THE HELL OUTTA DODGE, BABY! They'll be on to us pretty quick if they put two and two together and come up with you and me."

Two men came in the door. One was short, fat, wore a T-shirt— fitted right in. The other was a big , tall guy and wore a brown rumpled suit. Joe sensed a little drama— so he watched. He felt the four were connected.

When their eyes adjusted to the dim light, the two men glanced around and sure enough, headed toward the booth in the corner. They both stood facing Joe.

"Well, lookey here! Ain't this sweet! All cozy and all!"

"Right, and didn't invite us! Geez, I'm hurt! Here we was wantin' some grub, and come in here, and what do we find? Our two best buddies in all the world, out to lunch and didn't ask us! It pains me right here!" Fatso thumped his fist over his heart.

"Scoot over!" Big Guy slid in next to Blondie, Fatso plopped down by Fish Tie. Since Fatso and Fish Tie were the only ones facing Joe, he caught only their side of the conversation.

"Well, Lover-Boy, we seen you in your shiny new car. Made us wonder where in shit you got the dough for a ride like that!" Joe saw Fatso squint, then say "Ain't holdin' out on us are you? Hope not— 'cause if'n you are, you're DEAD MEAT!" He drew his finger across his neck. Blondie must have said something because Fatso leaned toward her, said "Do we look like golldang dummies? You're pullin' sumpin', all right! Where's the dough?"

Fish Tie said, "I been checkin' up on it. We ain't pullin' nuttin'!"

"Cut the shit!" said Fatso. "Get up! Hope you ain't ordered nuttin', 'cause we're leavin'!" Big guy must have said something, too, because Fatso leaned toward him said, "Shut up, Asshole! People'll be lookin'! C'mon! We're takin' a ride! If'n you try sumpin', I'll blow your golldang guts out! Get goin'!"

They all got up; Joe saw Blondie's purse slide to the floor. She reached for it, but Big Guy pushed her along. Fish Tie led the way with Fatso close behind. Joe suspected a gun was stuck in Fish Tie's back. He watched them leave in a rusted-out brown van headed west toward the river.

☠ ☠ ☠ ☠ ☠ ☠ ☠

Joe took the key out, pitched Lucy's purse under the counter, told the new girl, Sonja, he was leaving for a while. She looked perplexed— this was her first day and the place was full. He left driving east toward The Meadows apartment complex. It was in the opposite direction the van had gone.

☠ ☠ ☠ ☠ ☠ ☠ ☠

"Turn here!" Fred told Martin. They skidded to a stop, backed up, took an overgrown, weed filled road down to the river. They bumped along for a few minutes, then stopped.

"Get out," Fred said, "we'll walk from here."

Martin got out of the van, went around, slid the side door open. Fred pushed Lucy out, then opened the passenger door, cut the ropes holding Darrell to the seat. "Out, Asshole!"

"You got my damn feet tied. I can't!"

"Stick 'em out." Fred cut the ropes. "Easy now! Don't cause no trouble. Get over there with your girl friend. Here!" He pitched the rope over to Martin. "Tie his hands behind his back. Might as well tie hers, too— keep things simple." He pitched over the other piece of rope.

After they were tied up nice and safe, the four went deeper into the brush. They could hear the river sloshing against its bank. A steep cliff dropped off to the water below. Several sharp, pointed rocks stuck up. It was a long drop— and it looked pretty lethal.

"Stop! See that?" Fred said pointing down. "That's where the two of you are gonna be if'n you don't start talkin'!   Where's the dough?"

Lucy was bawling. Darrell didn't look too brave either. Martin moved toward Lucy. "Lemme whip it outta them!" he said. Lucy took a step back— her foot fought for solid ground— but didn't find it. She toppled backward over the cliff, screaming all the way down, then they heard the plop when she hit the rocks. All was quiet. Carefully, Martin looked over the side. She lay face up; he could tell she was dead— her neck looked broken. "0HHH JE-SUS!" he said. "SWEEEEET, JESUS, Fred! She's dead! What'll we do? 0h, God! 0h, God!"

"Shut up , Asshole! We didn't do nuttin'! For someone who acted so tough and wanted to waste somebody, you sure are takin' it bad!"

"0h, Lordy, Lordy! I ain't never killed nobody! Saw my Daddy dead in his hospital bed, my Granny in her casket, but I ain't never seen nobody DIE before!" He puked.

"Shit fire and save the matches! You make me sick!" Fred turned to Darrell who had his eyes closed, face crunched up and was sobbing. He had peed on himself— wetting the whole front of his slacks. "Hell! You ain't no better! Sobbing like a woman. If'n you don't tell me where that dough's at, I'll push you over with your girl friend." Fred moved toward him. " It's in an apartment. The Meadows— number twenty-seven," Darrell choked out. "Under the bed... in a suitcase." He fainted. Fred went over and kicked him in the leg— he didn't move. Bending down Fred cut the ropes on Darrell's hands, and told Martin to come on. The big man's color didn't look too good.

☠ ☠ ☠ ☠ ☠ ☠ ☠

Joe Cuppa reached The Meadows apartment complex, pulled his car into a space, turned on his hearing aid, and got out. He knew he had very little time, so he hurried along. He looked at the first door: ONE! "Shit!" he said and picked up his pace. He had been jogging along pretty good when, looking up, he saw number twenty-five, twenty-six and TWENTY-SEVEN. He climbed a flight of stairs, turned a corner and hurried toward the apartment. He slid the key into the lock— it opened easily— and slipped inside.

It was a small apartment— hardly any furniture. A chair and a TV were the only things in the living room. Down the hall were a small kitchen, bath and bedroom. He bent down, holding his sore ribs, reached under the unmade bed, pulled out the brown suitcase. He opened it, saw the money was inside. He shut it, hurried to the door, was about to open it, when he heard someone outside; they were fooling with the lock. He hurried back down the hall to the bedroom, jerked the window open, climbed out, shut it, and carrying the suitcase, eased his way around across the roof. He slid down a drain pipe, dropped to the ground and sprinted to his car. He pulled away about the same time Fred and Martin reached under the bed.

☠ ☠ ☠ ☠ ☠ ☠

Darrell came awake and sat up— he was confused. After a few seconds, things began to clear. He pushed himself up, plopped back down, got up more slowly. His legs shaking, he leaned against a tree. He knew he had wet his pants and after a few steps, found he'd also messed in them. Walking spraddle-legged, he peered over the cliff at Lucy. She still lay at the bottom. NO USE, he thought. SHE'S A GONER. Surprised and thankful he was still alive, he made his way back along the way he thought was right. Actually, he was going in the wrong direction.

☠ ☠ ☠ ☠ ☠ ☠

"Ain't a damn thing under there but dust bunnies!" Martin said, peering under the bed.

Fred got up, began searching the apartment. Martin stood up, put his hands on his hips, looked around the room. He went to the closet, opened it, but except for a few clothes, two pairs of shoes and a bowling ball, it was empty. The place was so sparsely furnished, with very few cabinets in the kitchen and bathroom to look in, it didn't take them long to know the money wasn't there. They stomped around on the carpet, cut open the mattress to make sure, then left heading back to the river.

☠ ☠ ☠ ☠ ☠ ☠

Darrell walked along the highway headed away from town. His slacks and underwear were wet where he had washed them in the river. His formerly shiny shoes were all scuffed up. A semi came barreling over a hill; he stuck out his thumb and the truck skidded to a stop just a little past him. He sprinted to the cab, climbed up, came face to face with one of the ugliest men he'd ever seen.

"Hey!" The man grinned, "I'm Greg Grover! If you think I'M UGLY, you should see my ol' lady— she's TEN TIMES uglier than me!"

Darrell hesitated for only a second. He figured anything was better than what was behind him. He closed the door.

"Where to Mack? I'm takin' a load of taters to Santa Fe. Take you that far, anyways. Let you off anywheres along the way."

"Thanks. Santa Fe'll be just fine."

"Pee-yoo, boy! You sure do stink! What'd you step in?" the driver asked, drawing back.

"Aw, I stepped in some dog-doo back there. Guess I didn't get it all off."

The man shifted the big truck's gears, went off down the road into the setting sun— taking his taters and Darrell to Santa Fe.

☠ ☠ ☠ ☠ ☠ ☠

When Martin and Fred got back to the cliff, they saw Darrell had gone. Looking over the side, they saw Lucy hadn't— she was still lying there. Following the trail Darrell had left, they discovered where he had taken a bath and washed his clothes. Not knowing what he had been doing, they thought he had crossed the river.

"This is where he went in. See any tracks commin' out?"

"Nah," Martin said, looking where they had tramped around mashing out Darrell's footprints. "Think he made it across?"

"Dunno. Dunno if he can swim or not. If'n he's over there, we gotta find him. There's a bridge a few miles down river and a road runs along the other side. Commone."

They got back in the van, bumped along the little road, pulled out onto the highway, came upon a semi stopped on the pavement.

"Look at that asshole!" Fred said. "Get that phone number on the back there! Some people ain't got no consideration for other folks! Here, write it down," he said handing Martin a ball-point, "I'll read it off. 1-800-FX-MYASS."

"I got it," Martin said. Fred pulled around the big truck, passed it. They didn't see Darrell in the cab— he noticed them, though, and was glad to see them speed on down the road out of sight. He settled back. He knew dark was nearly on them; they couldn't see him in the truck then. He remembered the money, his dog when he was ten, and Lucy. All were lost forever, but he was still alive. They passed houses, farms, a thick copse of trees and weeds where a couple days before, a green Jaguar had left the road. The car had sailed through the air, landed on its top. It wouldn't be found until fall, when all the leaves were off the trees. The man inside was dead, but had a lot of money on him. They wondered where he had gotten it, because, they discovered, he had never amounted to very much, and it was pretty certain he'd stolen it. In the long run, it didn't matter— the Sheriff and two deputies divided it among themselves. Winning a coin-toss with the District Attorney, the County Coroner took the diamond pinky ring.

☠ ☠ ☠ ☠ ☠ ☠ ☠

Joe Cuppa took the suitcase through the back door of the coffee house. He pushed it in under some shelves in the store room, arranged some boxes around it. Satisfied it was well hidden, left the room— not noticing a ragged boy hiding in a corner.

☠ ☠ ☠ ☠ ☠ ☠ ☠

Jason crawled out of the secret place, pushed aside the boxes, pulled the suitcase out. He dragged it over to the store room window. Leaving it there, he went out to the kitchen. He opened the refrigerator, took a gob of chicken salad in his hand, licked it off. Sucking his fingers, he went over to the stove, took the lid off a stainless steel pot. Balancing himself against the wall, he removed a shoe. He pulled off his sock, rolled it into a ball, dropped the dirty red rag into Joe Cuppa's pot of chili. He watched it bubble around for a while— it looked like a big red tomato.

Laughing, Jason tugged the suitcase down the street. He turned left at a corner, went down to a two-story brick house with a CON-DEMNED sign on the door. He dragged the suitcase up the stairs, over to the hole in the wall, shoved the scuffed-up old thing inside. He sat down with his back against the wall and waited for his ma, pa, brother and little sister to come home.

Scenes From a Murder
by Dirk Griffin

scene iv

in culinary richness
he moves serving
pleasure quietly
his life his own outside
these dark scents
heightened with sweetness
made full with the
thickness of cream

for change he
is silent
witness to
cravings
needs
and time

Dying to Write
by Ginny Fleming

It usually isn't this bad, Zake Williams thought, replacing the black cloth shrouding the body found in the alley behind the coffeehouse. *My guess is, the murderer was mighty pissed about something... I mean, this guy's dead six ways to Sunday. It appears he's been shot, stabbed, poisoned, garroted, mutilated, bludgeoned and suffocated. I'd say, someone wanted him dead in the worst way.*

"Detective Williams?" a petite blond woman slapped the short western-dressed policeman on the back. "You look like you're the guest of honor at a surprise party hosted by Stephen King." She chuckled, "You sure you'll be okay? Do I need to break out the smelling salts?"

He snorted sarcastically. "No, McMitchell. Keep your smelly salts to yerself. You're just chompin' at the bit to get your mitts on this guy. Ain't yuh, Doc? Guess your dance card's got an opening and this lucky stiff is yer new partner in the Dance Macabre. Well, hold yer horses. I'll release him when we're done here."

The medical examiner pulled on a pair of latex gloves, kneeled beside the corpse and quipped, "Don't get your jockeys in a knot. There's plenty I can do here before he's moved." She produced a large-sized thermometer. "Now that the photographer's done," she said, "what say you help me undo his slacks— and don't even think to accuse me of wanting to get into his pants. I need to get a core temp reading to determine the time of death."

Already wearing protective gloves, Williams unbuckled the dead man's bluejeans, pulling the tee-shirt up and exposing the corpse's abdomen for examination. He offered a quick assessment, "No trauma to the belly area—"

McMitchell suddenly thrust a meat thermometer through the dead man's stomach, an inch above the navel.

"You know?" Williams hissed, "Even though I know what's coming, I'm *never* ready for that. There's something about running a man through with the same device Momma Williams uses to roast turkey that, frankly, turns my stomach." He mimed sticking his finger down his throat and gagging.

"Cute." She snorted. "I'll bet you were a riot in junior high biology class. Probably dropped bugs down all the girls' dresses."

The short dark-haired man nodded solemnly. "Yep," he said, "and I had tiny mirrors strategically mounted on my shoes. Let me tell ya, I was BMOC in the boy's locker room. You know, Big Man On Campus."

Abruptly standing, the medical examiner brushed past Williams. "Well, I'd prefer you'd be a BMIC this evening." She quipped, "Go around front and be the Big Moron In the Coffeehouse. We need to get the goodies on Mr. Stiff-As-A-Board."

Zake raised a finger and opened his mouth, meaning to offer his usual smart-aleck southern-drawled retort; then thought better and silently headed toward the front entrance of the establishment.

"Coffee By George" occupied a choice location on the oldest street in New Albany, Indiana. Nestled between an attorney's office and a cult store dedicated to "Oz", the coffeehouse enjoyed a diverse clientele. Older, more sedate, customers mingled with Generation-X; the younger crowd in their retrograde `60's flower-power garb. This evening, the atmosphere was jovial as Williams walked in the front entrance. He glanced at the tiny bell tinkling over the door.

"Norm!!!" Everyone cheerfully called out in what Williams supposed was the traditional "George's" greeting.

"Norm my ass," the detective growled through his teeth, while smiling, nodding and giving a little wave. "What a *cheery* little caffine-junkie's paradise, this is." He spied a tall, bear of a man standing behind the counter. Zake estimated the man to be at least a head and a half taller than himself. "George?" he asked, flashing his badge and making his introduction.

"Guilty as charged," the dark-haired man chuckled, his eyes dancing a merry jig. "What can I do you for, Officer Williams? Latté, Cappuccino or Café au Lait?"

The short cowboy snorted, "How 'bout Corpse-a'la-Alley? Do you know there's a dead body behind your café?"

George swallowed and coughed out his nervous answer, "No—but, if you hum a few bars...."

"Droll." Williams sneered, "Do you serve your coffee with that smart-ass attitude?"

Shaking his head, the big man lowered his voice. "Sorry. Didn't mean nothin' by it. You just caught me by surprise. It's not everyday I'm told there's a dead body at my back door. Could we keep this quiet? Don't want to frighten the customers."

Another entering patron sounded the tiny bell over the door, and the coffee-revelers again cheerily called "Norm!!"

Zake nodded, "Fine and good. Can you show me through to the rear entrance?"

George sighed. "Dave?" he called. "Watch the register for me?" He motioned Williams into the back of the café. "Come on. Back door's this way. This isn't happening..." he shook his head in disbelief and opened the rear door, stepping into the alleyway before Williams. Glancing around at the working crime scene, George muttered, "Café doesn't need this kinda publicity."

"Aw, buck up, Little Buckaroo," Zake joked. Squatting beside the draped corpse, he drew the shroud down, exposing the dead man's face. "Know him?"

George nodded and ran his fingers through his thick black hair, "It's a little difficult, what with that rodent glue trap covering most of his face. But, that's Kenny Kendrick. Hangs around the café every once in awhile. Buggy guy. Jeee-sus! What happened to *him?*"

Turning his face up to the small-town coffee-baron, Zake studied the man for a moment. Finally, he said, "It appears, Mr. Kendrick had a sudden and violent attack of feelin' mighty poorly." Again, he pulled the shroud further away from the corpse, revealing the damaged torso, and the bloody shirt, "See the piano wire wrapped around his neck? Somebody garroted, stabbed, shot, razor-mutilated, poison-darted, suffocated and bludgeoned this poor slob. A dagger sticking outta him, a feathered dart alongside that... A bloody razor beside his right hand, that big ole rat trap shoved down over his nose and mouth... Plus, the bullet holes, not to mention the bludgeoning; apparently with this dark brown soda bottle, here. Looks like overkill to me." Zake shook his head. "You know if anyone disliked Mr. Kendrick enough to make him a Forensics Class Show and Tell?"

"No. Nobody comes to mind..."

Leaving a pair of paramedics to the task of bringing a stretcher alongside the body, McMitchell returned to Williams' side. "Any word?" she asked.

"Yes and no." The detective sighed, "George here, identified the corpus delicti as Kenny Kendrick. But, so far, he comes up a blank on our mega-dedicated murderer." Zake got to his feet. "Any suggestions, Doc?"

"I'll know more when I get this guy on the table," McMitchell said. "Right now, my guess is, he's been dead less than an hour and a half. Three at the most."

George blurted, "I opened the café about two hours ago!"

"Notice anything strange? See anything unusual?" Williams asked.

"No... Nothing out of the ordinary," the coffee-man shook his head. He chuckled, shaking his head again, "No, nothing strange... That is, unless you count the writers."

"Writers?" Williams and McMitchell united their voices in confusion.

George chuckled again, "Yeah, strange writers. Most of 'em women. They call themselves The Ohio Valley Bards and they meet here once a week."

Zake grinned, knowing the café owner had unwittedly lit McMitchell's feminist short fuse, and he mentally ticked off the microseconds until his medical examiner friend snorted, "Okay... So, where's the strange part come in?" She crossed her arms in front of her chest and tapped her foot.

"Hey! I didn't mean nuthin' by it!" the big man backed a step away from McMitchell. "It's just, if you saw this group, you'd say the same thing! I mean— Take tonight, for instance. They were all waiting for me to open the café."

The detective and the doctor both stared at the coffee-man like he was simple.

"No— No!" George chuckled, "You don't understand. They made me open the café early. When I arrived, they were all standing around in front. This was twenty minutes early, but I let them in, they went to their usual tables in the back, and... this is the unusual thing— suddenly, they got loud and then one of the women pestered me for a bottle of sarsaparilla."

"Scandalous!" Zake gasped sarcastically, "Imagine, asking you for a root beer! You should have called the cops right then and there!"

George snarled, *"Now* who's got the smart ass attitude? What I'm trying to tell you is, this woman didn't just *ask* me, she *pestered* me until I finally stopped what I was doing to fetch her a cold soda. Didn't want ice. In fact, as soon as she got her mitts on the bottle, she hurried out the front door. Five minutes later, she hurried back in an' joined the group for a flurry of whispering. Then, another writer scurried out the door and back again. This went on until after I flipped the "open" sign on the door, and my first actual customers trickled in. In and out, in and out, one writer after another— like I had a revolving door."

The medical examiner relaxed her tense stance, "And you say this was unusual behavior from this group?"

George laughed nervously, "Yeah... I really hate to speak ill of people, but they've been very strange, tonight. Even for them. I mean, Allison— the one who badgered me for the sarsaparilla, isn't the kind to be so demanding. But, tonight, she was practically rude."

"And, she was the first one out the door... and back in again." Zake lightly tapped his forehead, mentally "keying" the puzzle into his Michlelob-powered portable computer.

"Right," George nodded his head, "but, I'm sure Allison couldn't have anything to do with this," he indicated the corpse. "Allison is the sweetest woman... Practically shy. I don't think she'd squash a spider— even if it sat down beside her."

Zake chuckled, "A regular Little Miss Muffet, huh?"

"No... No, more like a female Saint Francis of Assisi. Gentle with all God's creatures. Always a smile and a kind word. Very pleasant and calm. *Usually."*

"Just not tonight?" McMitchell asked. The look in her eyes told Williams she'd already processed the two plus two riddle and was close to arriving at a preliminary answer. "Where are these writers now?"

"Inside. In their usual place in the back. They'll be there..." he checked his watch, "about twenty minutes more."

Turning to her smart aleck partner, the doctor nodded her head toward the café. "Are you pondering what I'm pondering?" she said.

"I think so, Brain!" the cowboy gave his best imitation of the genial cartoon mouse. "But," he continued, "wouldn't it be better to wash your hands before you try to take over the world? Narff! Poit!!"

"Hush, Pinky," the woman supplied the refrain, "or I'll be forced to hurt you." The two friends headed toward the front of the coffeehouse, George on their heels.

"What're you gonna do?" he asked his shorter companions. "You gonna interrogate the whole café?" The mismatched trio entered the front door, causing the tiny bell to tinkle.

"Norm!!"

"What the hell?!?" McMitchell laughed.

Zake snarled good-naturedly, "Ignore them. Too much caffeine. They all think they're in Boston."

Leading the investigators to a tiny room set in the back of the café, George indicated a group of people sitting at small round tables shoved together, forming a misshapen singular desk. "Officers," he said, "these are The Ohio Valley Bards. Uh... Bards, this is Officer Williams and Doctor McMitchell, County Medical Examiner. They'd like to ask you all a few questions." George introduced each "Bard" in turn, going around the tables until he arrived at a slight woman with salt and pepper hair and a pronounced demure presence. "...and this is Allison McKinsy," he ended his hospitable chore. "This is the Bard's weekly meeting. They—"

"We're about to leave." The Bard known as Jesse interrupted their host, "Meeting's over. Time to go. Great night, George. See ya next week? Same bat time; same bat channel." She stood from her seat and moved towards the register.

Zake blocked her path, his hands on his hips, cowboy fashion. She towered over him by a head span. "Hold on, Bard." He growled through a cynical smile. "A few questions. "Know a guy named Kenny Kendrick?"

Jesse sent daggers at the short man standing between herself and escape. "Could be," she snarled, "I know a lot of guys... *Some* from the coffeehouse."

"Did I *say* Kendrick was from the coffeehouse?" Williams grinned.

"Well, you didn't say he *wasn't* from the coffeehouse!" she snipped.

The lone man of the group stood from the table and hissed at the detective, "I'll have to ask you to put a halt to all these questions until I can confer with my clients—"

"Are you an attorney?" McMitchell interrupted.

A furious blush blazed across the man's face and he abruptly took his seat, "No... I read a lot of Grisham and I write legal suspense. But, I've enrolled in prelaw for accurate research."

"Well, research this, Counselor," Zake snarled, pointing his index finger at the man. "A man was killed behind the café tonight. What do you know about it?"

"Uh-uh-uh... Nothin'. Nothin' at all."

Zake grinned. "Nothin', huh?" he leaned across the table, glaring at the man and growling. "You wouldn't be holding back on us, now... *would ya?*"

Suddenly, the demure woman sitting under a small cuckoo clock leaped to her feet and screamed, "I can't take this pressure!! All the accusations!! All the relentless grilling!! All the... *violence!!* I confess— I did it! *I killed Kenny Kendrick!"*

Without missing a beat, the others raised their hands in unison and chanted in a loud chorus, *"We ALL killed Kenny Kendrick!!"*

The whole café fell silent.

A woman with long red, feathered and beaded hair, broke the silence by snorting an evil cackle, "Yeah, that's right! We *all* did it!! We *all* killed Kenny Kendrick!! Now, are you gonna make something of it?!?"

"You bet yer beads, Pocahontas!" Williams moved his accusing finger, pointing it in the sassy woman's direction, "I'm gonna make something of it, all right. All you Bards are taking a ride downtown."

"Godammit! Can't we all just get along for once?" offered a woman dressed entirely in black leather.

A silver-haired boisterous female Bard sneered, "Nasty man deserved everything he got!! Nasty man!!"

The writer George earlier introduced as Felicity, the group artist, quipped, "You got that right, Joyce. The creep."

"That'll teach him to annoy women!" A petite writer, wearing a golden necklace spelling out the name "Linda", joined in the man-bashing.

Zake shook his head in disgust. He growled, "Load up, people."

George cleared his throat, "Excuse me— You're taking them all downtown? Right now? This minute? All the Bards? You can't do that!!"

This time, McMitchell was the one to snort laughter. "One step back, Coffee-Boy," she said. "Williams may look small, but I promise you, his bite is way worse than his bark. If the detective says these fiction peddlers are taking the redeye to the station— then, they're already booked in the paddywagon."

"No problem!" George raised his hands palms up, backing away from the tiny imposing woman. "I just wondered if they'd be allowed to settle their tabs first; that's all!"

Zake laughed, "Of course. I can even make it an order." He glanced at the writers and snarled, "Bards? Pay the good innkeeper— and don't forget to leave a big ole hefty tip! Comprende?"

Much low-level grumbling accompanied The Ohio Valley Bards as they lined up at the counter to settle their nightly bill, handing the money to Dave at the register. After ringing the sixth Bard through, and witnessing each drop a five spot in the tip jar, the bemused waiter turned to a forlorn George rinsing a cup in the bar sink. "What's going on?" Dave chuckled. "They all look like they've signed up for a death march."

George coughed into his hand and murmured, "Kenny Kendrick was found murdered in the alley. The policeman, here, is taking the Bards downtown for questioning, and—"

"Oh, my God!! They've killed Kenny!! *You bastards!!*" Dave gasped in horror, both hands held to his lips.

"Remember." Zake grinned, "Innocent until proven *they ba-a-d-d.*" He ushered the grumbling writers out the front door, as he called for backup on his cellular phone.

Dave looked to his boss still cleaning the cup at the sink. "You know?" the waiter shook his head, "I believe our Thursday nights will be a little quieter for awhile."

☠ ☠ ☠ ☠ ☠ ☠ ☠

Three weeks passed. The bell over the door at "Coffee by George" tinkled in the cool evening air. *"Norm!!"* came the familiar welcome.

"Norm, my ass." Williams snarled though a genial smile, "I got yer

Norm right here."

McMitchell chuckled, strolling through the door behind him, "Zake, give it a rest. You know, somewhere, deep inside, you'll always be Norm, to me." She ushered her short western-dressed friend to the coffeehouse's back room, strangely empty on a Thursday night. She held up two fingers to the dark-haired man towering over her. "George?" She smiled, "Bring us two Milky Ways and two large orders of your chicken and dumplings."

"We're out of chicken and dumplings," George shook his head, his pencil poised over an order pad.

"Okay..." McMitchell mused, perusing a menu, "bring us Mocha Mints. And two large orders of chicken and dumplings."

"I said, we're outta chicken and dumplings."

"Fine." The pretty blond nodded her head, "How'bout, Caramel Cappuccinos... And two large orders of chicken and dumplings."

"Listen, Doc—" George pointed his pencil at the medical examiner.

"And you thought I was the difficult one." Williams grinned, "George, be a pal. Bring us something made from a dead bird— preferably cooked. And two Milky Ways."

"Gotcha, Detective." George handed the order slip to Dave and took a seat beside the two officers. "So, what's the skinny on the Bards. Did they do it, ya think?"

"Funny thing, George." Williams leaned back in his chair and said, "The whole thing was one big accident. You see, the writers were having a little writer exercise. Each one was to bring a weapon for the perfect murder. Just a "show and tell" thing, you understand. But, Allison didn't want to participate with the rest of the group. She's a rabid pacifist, doesn't believe in violence of any kind, even fictional. Didn't want to be a part of this particular exercise. So, she got upset, jumped up, badgered you for the sarsaparilla, and left the café, intent on driving home."

Dave brought the doctored-up coffees and Zake paused while stirring his frothy drink.

"So, anyway," he continued, "like I said, Allison left upset. She hurried around to the side street, where she'd left her car. Just as she was unlocking her Camry, someone grabbed her shoulder. Natural reaction caused her to swing and bash her assailant with the soda bottle. It was Kenny; we've no idea what his motive was for scaring the lady. 'Fraid we'll never know for sure, 'cause he staggered into the alley and collapsed. Allison followed him, and determined, rightly or not, that the man was dead from the head wound she'd caused. She then rushes back into the café, tells her pals, and they hatch a plan. Everyone wants to help their hysterical friend. So, they, one by one, leave by the front door with their chosen weapons and add further abuse to a man who's never gonna lay his hand on another innocent woman in this lifetime."

"That's bizarre!!" George shook his head, "You know? If it'd been any other group, you'd never get me to believe that story. It's a strange world. So, what's gonna happen to the Bards now?"

"Too soon to tell," Zake took a bite of the turkey sandwich Dave set in front of him, chewed and garbled around the food. "My guess..." he swallowed, "and this is just a guess, mind you. Allison will get off with probation. I can't see any judge or jury mean enough to send that sweet lady away. And the rest of the Bards? I'd say, they're goin' up river for a few. But, that's not a bad thing, not totally. They all claim to never have time to write— Now they'll have oodles of time. And we know, they're all just dying to write."

Scenes From a Murder
by Dirk Griffin

scene v

and so the car
red with anger
calls him to the road
filled with business
he obsesses on possessions
seeking ownership
not experience
speed accelerating
beyond feeling
speed a balm
against worry
he presses the pedal
as if squashing a bug
and hurries

scene vi

what do they seek
amid dark rich roast
what is this companionship
found in a warm stimulating beverage
is it the sweetness of too much sugar
the cream cooling the darkness
or is it some social voyeurism
looking silently into
other lives over the
rim of a cup

Renewable Resource
by Jeannine Baumgartle

Every day I kill him
(without malice, of course)
and the next morning
he's back, the same
little crinkled brown
spider.
He likes the heat light,
I guess, and the warm
moist corner by the tub,
suspended there quietly
on the single strand
he was able to spin.
Every day, before
wrapping him in kleenex,
I tell him we have
a nice dark basement,
out of the way of
compulsive housewives,
but he must prefer it
here, at least enough
to die every day.

JAVACISE
By Marla Bilbrey

Life's too short for bad coffee, especially when our country's anthem is now: "One nation, with liberty, large fries, and a coffee to go!" Plus, the only exercise most of us get is; "*Javacise*," you know, that burst of motion after spilling coffee in someone's lap, and the only REAL flying saucer is when the plate that was supposed to be under the cup goes flying across the room as a result. If we are not "*Javacising*," then we try to exercise by pushing our luck. Frank took it like a man and blamed it on his wife's "fowl" luck.

"Have a nice day!"

"No thanks. I have other plans."

Lola picked up the skimpy tip left by the customer. ""Lousy jerk" she muttered. As Eliot says, "*I'm tired of measuring out my life by coffee spoons*," she thought as she placed the tableware in the tub.

Working for the coffeehouse since its opening, she had seen many people come and go. Frank did not like her working here. Thought she was becoming too close to some of the patrons. The tips were decent enough, she guessed. The job was easy, keep the cups full, show some leg, a bit of cleavage, stay out of the way of the ones on a caffeine binge, and flip mouse turds out of the way when no one was looking.

Frank suspected that Lola was having an affair. He had heard her coo-ing about some man named Pete to her sister. She liked to grow her own herbs, and was into alternative healing. She made her own medicines and herbal drinks. For some reason she liked placing some sort of mint in her bra to encourage Pete to come on to her. Any man that fell for that sort of tom-foolery had to be a pussy! Frank had no idea how to compete with such as that. He thought the clientele at the coffeehouse was a bit too weird for him. Especially since Lola sizzled with her looks, and that body. If that wasn't enough to drive a man crazy, then that guy needed more than a bunch of herbs to turn him on! One benefit of being married to a weed junkie was the mighty fine smokes she rolled from her country-side gatherings. He still couldn't figure out why she took so many spearmint leaves to work. She had told him she liked to sprinkle them all over the coffeehouse floor.

☒ ☒ ☒ ☒ ☒ ☒ ☒

The thief huddled next to the counter by the cash register. Eyes red from the cast of the street light outside the door. Sitting very still as if to "sniff" the air.

"I see you, you rodent!" thought Pete. Not making a sound, Pete moved cautiously among the tables. Bits of cookie littered the floor, and brown sticky spots pulled at his feet where patrons had spilled their coffee the previous evening.

"Ah. Yes. Sit and contemplate your life, you morsel stealing grab-ber! Wait there and I'll give you a reason to wish you'd thought more tonight on your life!" he thought.

Pete maneuvered around the last table, and pounced upon his prey. Nails grabbing, he sank his teeth into the neck, tearing out a great gash, blood flowed upon the floor. As he chewed, he settled down to a night of eating. "No one, and I do mean no one, trespasses in my store!" he exclaimed.

☒ ☒ ☒ ☒ ☒ ☒ ☒

"PETE! Hey, Pete! Come on, where are you? Your Latté is ready."

Larry placed the cup on the table closest to the cash register. "Dang, Pete! I wish you would stay off the counters! Left your footprints again! What do ya do, boy? Dance up here?"

Larry picked up the broom and dustpan to sweep the litter on the floor. "Ah, Pete. You knocked over chairs again. Man. I wish you'd be a bit more careful. These things cost MONEY! You must have had some party last night, dude. You better hope that your friends have all left! I am so tired of up righting these chairs you knock over. Look, buddy, you felled three of them last night! Man!"

As Larry's hand moved over the back of the chair, the curve of the wood reminded him of Lola's thighs. Rock hard and smooth as silk. He would like to fire Pete, but the female patrons of the coffeehouse

all loved Pete, thought he was cute. And cuddly. The cuddly part is what the ladies found the most amusing about Pete. He had no qualms about crawling on some woman's lap, batting at her breasts while he sat there nuzzling under her chin, pawing at her genitals. The women just giggled at him and his antics. Larry wished that the women would let him do the things that Pete got to do. Especially that "hot one" Lola! Pete went crazy over her breasts! Larry wished she was a pillow that he could rub and roll on all over.

Leaning on the broom, Larry brought to mind how Lola and Pete acted last night before closing time. She had the biggest breasts he had ever seen, and Pete got to rest his head against them. Her long red hair flowing down in silky waves. The unfairness of life, Lola's large red lips kissing Pete's scrawny whiskery mouth, her arms wrapped around him, pressing him close to her.... Pete's attitude while looking at Larry, as if to say, "I feel great! I don't kiss bad either...."

He put his thumbs in the waistband of his pants pulling the material away from his body, gyrated his hips to get his trousers back up where they had slid down, pulled at his crotch to adjust the fit, then picked at his seat. "Gotta quit thinking about her. All that would lead to is trouble. Pete's my pal, if he can cop-a-feel off of THAT one, why should I care?" Larry shrugged.

"PETE!" he yelled.

As he stretched and yawned, Pete slowly rose from where he rested, his "bed" located in the small nook behind the counter, where the clean wash cloths were kept. It had been a long night, with not as much action as Larry spouted off about. If Larry wanted to know exactly what happened last night, IF Larry wanted things differently HE could protect the store.

"*Ah, cool. Didn't clean the blood off right here.*" Pete slowly licked the spot of blood he missed in his night's cleaning. "*It's a poor cook that can't lick his own fingers,*" he thought. Remembering the action of the hunt, he settled back down, eyes rolled back in his head to dream about his victory.

"There you are, boy! Come on, drink your stuff. We open soon and we have a lot of work to do!"

Pete opened one eye, looked at Larry, and turned over to go back to sleep.

"Well, if you are going to sleep in, at least move your butt so I can get a dishrag to wash up."

The tinkle of the bell over the door announced the first customer of the day. Jumping off the towels, Pete ran toward the front of the shop.

"Hey, Pete, SLOW DOWN! Dang it you are like a Chihuahua on amphetamines!"

☠ ☠ ☠ ☠ ☠ ☠

"Momma, what happened to Poppa? He didn't come home last night", asked Willie.

"Honey, Poppa went to work and didn't show up later. It's not like Poppa to not come home." Momma picked up a few bits of cloth and placed them on her Willie's bed, her teeth chattering, hands fidgety.

Willie was the last of her children at home, which was located between the coffeehouse and the craft shop. The other kids had already taken up residence along the row of shops on the old street. Every now and then she would see them scurrying along between the shops. Some of her girls were now mommas, tending to their own broods. Their mortality rate had increased lately since Pete moved into the coffeehouse. No one could yet prove he was the one killing them, but as soon as enough proof was collected, there would be a trial among the members of the Baseboard Committee, and then the judgement!

☠ ☠ ☠ ☠ ☠ ☠

"ORDER! Please! We must come to order!"

The Baseboard Committee huddled in Momma's home for the weekly meeting. All the families' heads of household were represented. Some were white-haired, a few gray, several black, but most were brown. During the crisis they were experiencing, the rats were very co-operative. The mice seemed to not mind crowding up a bit to accommodate the presence of the larger rodents.

"Another one of us disappeared last night. Momma Mouse reported that Poppa went shopping in the coffeehouse and did not return. Millard Mouse looked over the place this morning and found a blood sample and a few hairs that we believe to have belonged to Poppa Mouse.

"Last week, one of the members of the Alley Alliance saw Pete

take a member of the Squirrel Tree Family and devour him. The next day, a mole was dug up on the sidewalk, entrails apparently eaten. The evidence is mounting up that the one doing the killing is Pete.

"The Chair members of the Scientific Mice Board have given me their recommendations on how we can capture Pete and bring him to trial. While this method can work, we will need the co-operation of all the members and families here. As you know, some of us won't make it, we will have to be willing to offer ourselves up as bait, to catch him.

"Millard Mouse, are you ready to present your ideas for the Base-board Committee to vote on?"

Millard, the representative of the Rafters Society, took the podium.

☠ ☠ ☠ ☠ ☠ ☠ ☠

Pete lay on the floor under the table watching the mouse hole located next to the ladies restroom, and the one next to the door jam. Slowly he waved a sprig of anise back and forth, the smell wafting in the air. He could hear a lot of scurrying behind the walls, and could tell they were talking to one another but couldn't understand what they were saying. *"Ah, well"* thought Pete, *"if I can't get one of them tonight, I guess I'll have to eat that food Larry put out for me. Why can't they make mouse-flavored cat food?"* he pondered.

"YEOOOW!" screeched Pete as Lola stepped on his tail.

The screech startled Larry, upsetting the tray of drinks he was carrying. "Dang it, Pete! Get out of here!" he hollered.

"Don't blame the cat, Larry! What would YOU do if someone stepped on YOU! Oh, Pete, honey, I am so-oo sorry! Come here my precious little baby," she said bending over to scoop Pete up into her arms.

Larry caught a side view of her body knifing over to get Pete. He saw her red bra peek from her low cut shirt, the creamy mounds spilling forth, while at the same time seeing the slit up the side of her skirt open to get a tiny glimpse of the satin garter belt.

"Oh-man-oh-man-oh-man!" grunted Larry under his breath as he adjusted the sudden tightness in his trousers.

☠ ☠ ☠ ☠ ☠ ☠ ☠

"The Scientific Mice Board has discovered the hair and blood samples do belong to Poppa Mouse. We also have proof that the saliva belonged to Pete. We need to vote on the measures of judgement pronounced by the board and committee, to proceed or not."

"All in agreement, signify by saying 'Aye!'"

The mice and rats rose as if one, the shout of "Aye!" reverberating throughout the walls.

"The vote is unanimous! Let us proceed with Plan A."

☠ ☠ ☠ ☠ ☠ ☠

Pete jumped, hearing a high-pitched squealing sound grating on his ear drums. Burying his head in Lola's breasts, his arms rapidly made rowing motions over his head and ears as if to remove the sound from his head.

"What's up buddy?" cooed Lola. "Larry, you sure you won't let me have Pete?"

"Sure, Lola. I keep telling you, go out with me and then you can have Pete. Let me have a chance at what Pete gets to do and I'll give you what ever you want!"

"Not on your life, Larry! I'll steal Pete first!"

You do that Lola. Yes, you do that. You do that, and I'll be talking right sweetly with you. You understand? You do that and I'll make sure I get what I want, thought Larry. Larry licked his lips, and said, "I wouldn't advise you doing that Lola."

☠ ☠ ☠ ☠ ☠ ☠

The members of the Baseboard Committee scurried around the shops getting the materials together for the night raid against Pete. The rats busied themselves preparing the inside of the coffeehouse.

☠ ☠ ☠ ☠ ☠ ☠

Lola tugged at the spandex black pants to get them over her hips, tucking the tight turtleneck sweater into the pants. Next, she wrapped her long red hair into a loose bun to hide it inside the black toboggan. She checked her bag. *Ah! Yes, I have the aconite, the jimsonweed, and the herb called broom*, she thought. Her high heels clicked as she hurried over to open the door.

☠ ☠ ☠ ☠ ☠ ☠

Frank peered into the window of the coffeehouse. No one there that he could see. Taking a suction cup out of his jacket pocket, he pressed it against the window. With his other hand he took the cutter and etched a circle around the plunger.

☒ ☒ ☒ ☒ ☒ ☒ ☒

Pete picked up the anise sprig with his teeth. Silently creeping to the mouse hole, he waved the herb around, hoping it would entice the small mice out. *Always like to start with a small appetizer*, he thought.

☒ ☒ ☒ ☒ ☒ ☒ ☒

Larry slipped out of the bathroom, thinking he heard a noise. *If it's that danged cat, I'll hang his hide*, he thought.

☒ ☒ ☒ ☒ ☒ ☒ ☒

Frank lowered the glass circle, laying it aside; he reached into the hole and unleashed the latch that locked the window. A slight screeching sound erupted as he shoved the window up. Larry, grabbing a flashlight, threw a dishrag over the bulb to dim the beam and proceeded to the back of the shop.

☒ ☒ ☒ ☒ ☒ ☒ ☒

The anise smell wafted through the air. Millard shoved Willie toward the hole, while Willie signaled the rats to move forward, the squirrels scurrying up the rafters, mouths bulging.

☒ ☒ ☒ ☒ ☒ ☒ ☒

Lola took her key and opened the back door. Peeking in, seeing no one, she stepped inside and clicked the door shut. As she turned, she bumped into Larry.

"I see you decided to come over and play a game with me after all Lola." he said, grabbing her behind.

"Oh, gosh Larry! Let me go! Please let me go!"

"What have we here, Lola? A bag? More of your wacko herbs? Hee hee, let me have some of that!"

"Larry, please. Let me go and I'll leave and we'll pretend we weren't here!"

"You came over to ME!" Larry said, as he tugged the toboggan off her head, and the red hair tumbled down. Gathering a fistful, he brought her mouth to crush against his. He bit her bottom lip, forcing her mouth open, then jabbed his tongue rapidly into her mouth. She tried not to gag.

"AH! I knew it! You sleaze bag whore! And it's with LARRY! You both over there!" Frank said, motioning them over to the counter.

"Frank, please, it ain't what you think!"

"Shut up," he said while walking towards the bathroom door. As he moved, he stepped on Pete's tail, sending the cat into a frenzy. As Frank tried to get out of the feline's way, he tripped and toppled into Larry's arms.

"Sorry buddy," Larry said as he caught Frank, "I ain't into MEN!" and knocked him to the floor. "Get over there by your slutty wife."

☠ ☠ ☠ ☠ ☠ ☠ ☠

Frank and Lola huddled next to each other, her purse spilled out on the floor. The ceiling fan made a steady swish-swish sound above them. Larry flipped the bag over and saw the herbs in their plastic bags, the packet of cigarette papers lying there.

"Well, Lola BA-BY! Roll me and Frank a smoke will ya? I think we need to party before I get what I want!"

Lola, stifling a chuckle, agreed and grabbed her bag and laid out what she'd need. She proceeded to produce two nice big joints for the guys.

☠ ☠ ☠ ☠ ☠ ☠ ☠

Willie rubbed spearmint leaves all over his body, hoping the repugnant smell would diffuse the attraction of the anise in the air. He went to the hole and peeked out at Pete.

"Here, mousey! Com' on bud, come here!" Pete said, trying to entice the mouse out.

☠ ☠ ☠ ☠ ☠ ☠ ☠

Larry lit the two joints, handed one to Frank. Both men drew heavily on the smoking tubes, chest making little heaves as they held the smoke in.

The mice quickly took the fishing line and pulled it through the pulleys the rats had hammered in. All the large rodents stood ready to

hold the guidelines. Willie stayed close to the hole to let Pete know he was there.

☠ ☠ ☠ ☠ ☠ ☠ ☠

The joints glowed as Larry and Frank sucked them down. Each man's eyes watered from the harshness of the raw smoke. The herbs affected their senses almost immediately. Heart rates increasing, while their minds distorted what they actually saw. Lola waited patiently for her chance to grab Pete and escape.

Willie made sure the noose was in place before he decided to run out of his hole, the squirrels above ready to bombard Pete with nuts if things didn't go quite right.

Running out of the entrance and down the side of the wall, he squealed to signal to all that the game had begun.

Pete dropped the sprig and took chase, claws out and swatting at the small mouse. With each downward swoop, the rodents squealed, "JUMP!" Willie felt the WHOOSH of air behind the force of the paw coming down and leapt. The squirrels dropped their ammunition to slow the cat down a bit. Racing through the table legs, Pete followed close behind.

"Look! That cat! Go Pete!' Larry exclaimed.

Frank jerked around, trying to catch a glimpse of the man Lola was so crazy about.

Pete spun around the table leg and headed into the noose, as Willie cleared it a slight second before the cat. The rats pulled hard on the line. The nylon string caught around the feline's neck, and they pulled him up into the air.

"That cat is flying!" both men exclaimed. Lola caught her hands to her chest, not realizing what was happening. Pete's hands went for his throat to get the line off of himself, his legs gyrating like a wind-mill, swinging in the air.

"DUCK!" screamed Larry as Pete whirled across the room.

"Ah, shee-it! Where's the duck!" said Frank as he scrambled un-der a nearby table.

Kicking hard, Pete swung toward Larry, nails out to grab onto some-thing to stop his motion. "He's after me! I swear Pete! I'll be good to you boy, I promise!" The added excitement sent Larry's blood pressure soaring, and with the effects of the broom, aconite and jimsonweed in his blood stream, his heart exploded. Quaking and thumping on the floor, Frank went berserk. "You witch! You witch! What sort of spell have you cast on us?" he yelled at Lola.

Lola stood up and looked right at Frank and said, "You touch me and you'll be next! You hear me!"

Taking a chair from one of the tables, she scooted it across the floor to where Pete was swinging. Over her shoulder, she said to Frank, "If you stay calm Frank, you may live. Shut up and let me get Pete, and we'll all be out of here." As she reached up to grab Pete, Frank kicked her chair leg. Loosing her balance, she grabbed the cord that adjusted the speed of the fan, while with her other hand she grasped Pete's leg. The combination of her hand holds, and her body weight, caused the noose to tighten more on Pete's neck. As she fell, the line sliced through his neck, decapitating him instantly.

She tumbled off the chair, her head hit the corner of a table, and killed her. The blood mingled in her red hair. The table rebounded by sending its contents flying throughout the room. Cups and saucers were airborne.

"OH GOD! The aliens are invading!" Frank screamed as he rolled into a ball under the table, the plates crashing around him.

The rodents quickly rolled the fishing line up, and tucked it in a mouse hole for another day.

Frank trembled under the table, watching the rodents scurry around the floor, Lola's blood pooling next to him. Pete's eyes staring right at him, Larry's body releasing its fluids. That wasn't so bad. Neither was the headless hairy body the rats were carrying off. Or the broken spaceships. He could see these enemies.

What the police couldn't figure out was his screaming, "It's that damn duck that did it! She brought that DUCK in and that's when it got REALLY bad!"

Scenes From a Murder
by Dirk Griffin

vii

the aromas of warmth
are shattered by an explosion
followed with the sounds
of a thousand wind chimes
screaming in a storm
one by one the patrons
fall from their perches
crying in fear
crying in their mortality
then the cold invades
first a blast of winter air
chilling beyond their fear
followed by the white and
rushing snow
blowing furiously in
through the shattered
remains of the window
'offe' in red and yellow
letters hang in desperation
to the frame
as the thunder finds distance
in echoes of its wrath

slowly sensing the danger's
passing people rise
looking for signs of the
angry invasion
they find a beauty
red staining her dark hair
her deep eyes wide
with the horror of
her last moment

It's All In How You Look At It
by Jeannine Baumgartle

We are all murderers, you know. Even me.

It all began with my Aunt Rilda, when she was a teenager (my Mom is that much older than her which is how I know, plus she had me young). They had a portrait made of Rild at age twelve, that's how neat everybody thought she was. —The only family member to have one. It still hangs over the fireplace in my grandma's house, even though it's warped a little over the years.

One of the earliest things I remember was being compared to Rilda, who seemed more like an older cousin than an aunt. She was a "real" Christian and didn't yell or get angry like the rest of us. I never could see what she had to get angry about. All the family loved her and whatever she did was right (whether I thought so or not). But Mom didn't buy into my complaining:

"Families are sort of like one person, sweetheart. When you reject one member, you reject the whole group. Our life is in our relationships and if those fail..." She hesitated, looking me over. "You know math. A negative and a positive cancel each other out. You be the positive."

I turned that over once and relaxed. In effect she was saying I was only in charge of myself. And I could do positive.

I think we were all taken by surprise that year when Aunt Rilda changed religions and got engaged suddenly to Foley Page, West 9th's equivalent of the town drunk. There was this horrible transition for the whole family which somehow worked its way into acceptance, of sorts. It was like accepting her death, since we'd probably never see her again. She and Foley were moving to Texas where they would stay with a cousin of his till they could find work and get a place of their own.

Somehow we all got through the shower and wedding and reception, and I stayed out of it as much as possible, not having much to say that anybody'd want to hear. Besides, kids weren't allowed at the wedding. We were brought out afterward for a piece of cake, and to wave and throw rice as the couple headed for the car. That was when I first noticed the mind nail sticking out from my mom's head about two inches above her left temple. Nobody else saw it, so I worried it was just me going crazy. But every time I looked over, there her hand would be, almost touching that nail as if she felt a headache coming on. We cleaned up the hall and went home. I kept thinking about Aunt Rilda and how she might be doing with her new husband, so far away.

We're pretty much in our old summer routine again. I get up in the morning and help hang the wash on the line. The grass is still pretty wet then and our shoes get soaked. Mom shivers. Every time she leans over the clothes basket her hand goes up to where there's only about an inch of that nail still showing, and she swallows like she's going to be sick.

So it goes. My little brother gets the pans out of the stove drawer for her and Dad works outside when he gets home, trying to fix the roof quietly. There was a phone call from Grandma the other day. I have a new cousin. That pleased us all. Life is reassuring; we needed that.

☠ ☠ ☠ ☠ ☠ ☠

I realize now I will never be all I should be. Everybody needs too much. My little brother needs a Mom. Dad holds down two jobs to pay hospital bills. And the gray lady that lies in bed in the back room needs to get well. I take in her tray, the window by the bed not really giving us much light. She sits up, tries to eat. There is only the flat head of the nail showing now. I avoid looking at it, concentrate instead on holding the glass for her, tipping it just so, so she won't choke when she drinks. Help her to the bathroom after, our heads close together, so close I think I could maybe...if I was careful, slip a fingernail under that blunt gray nail head— The phone rings. Mom's seated now, so I go take care of it. Another solicitor of course. I'm too frustrated to think how to get rid of him. Mom is waiting for me, needing to get back to bed.

☠ ☠ ☠ ☠ ☠ ☠

Afternoon. I think I'll just check on her, but really I know what I'm going to do. That mind tack has to come out— I'll combine that with smoothing the hair away from her face, work a couple of fingernails under the rim, nudge it loose, ease it out. I stand in the doorway a minute, draw in a slow breath. Tip-toe toward her, loving, reverent; powerful too, in the intensity of my mission. I will have my mother back, my little brother's mother too, and give Dad back his wife.

Standing there barefoot on the board floor, I reach out, suddenly pull back. It's gone. The mind nail, I can't see it... Reach out again and touch coolness... She's peaceful now, pale and peaceful, the strained look gone from her face. I seem to be in a vacuum, nothing to think or do...

That's it. I hunt up my shoes, jamb them on and walk down to the coffee house to get Dad. That's where he stops between jobs. He looks up when I come in, puts down his cup, his brown eyes filling with what I don't have to say.

At home my little brother is a nuisance, wanting somebody to cry on, but Dad takes care of him. I'm busy writing this, which I will send to my Aunt Rilda.

We are all murderers, you know. Even me.

A Little "Sugar" Could Cover It Up
By Elizabeth J. Gross.

I went to a coffeehouse— a place I'd never been before.
I saw it was very dim inside— when entering thru the door.
In a darkened corner across the smoky room,
I saw my cheating boyfriend with I know not whom.
As I watched he rose and spoke so softly to his paramour,
Then headed toward the restroom across the café's floor.
Quickly, I reached deep down inside a little silken bag,
Then with vial in my hand, I whispered "Harlot" to the hag!
And before this wanton slut had any time to stop and think,
I poured a healthy dose of hemlock into HIS amber drink.
I then ran into the ladies room, and huddled by the sink,
And peeking thru the crack, I saw him take a drink.
I rushed home in my car— giggling all the way,
So hyped-up, proud of what I had done this day!
When I opened my front door— I could celebrate no further,
For seated on my couch, was my boyfriend and his mother!
Where had I been, he asked, for I had invited them to dinner!
There was an edge to his voice— he sounded very bitter.
Suddenly they became concerned, as I turned a nasty pale.
Images sprang in front of me going off to jail!
They came closer to me and kindly asked about my health.
I was so very sick you see— I'd poisoned someone else!
Again!

Scenes From a Murder
by Dirk Griffin

scene viii

he brushes past the blue
uniforms and yellow tape
to see what he knows will
be waiting

no one believes him when
he says
there is a sameness in death
but he knows from experience
our independence
our lives
our hopes
are merely dressings
that lose meaning
in the first moment
we fail to live

witnesses speak
never with the same story
all their observations centering
on themselves
who would notice
who could look beyond
their lives to see another
losing theirs

in the end there are only stories
and chalk hieroglyphics marking
a life lost
and a search for why
a search for truth
found in death
denied the living

Yankee Java
by Marian Allen

She stepped into the coffee shop, cool in a white linen suit, a silver lamé clutch purse tucked under her arm. She paused just inside the door, crossed the room and slid into a booth.

The waiter, a slim young man dressed in casual chic, approached.

"What'll it be?"

"Cappuccino." She smiled suddenly, touched each end of the table, and said, "Put up a whole row of them, starting here and ending here."

The waiter smiled back and said, "We will begin with one."

Alone again, she fished smoking gear from her purse and lit a cigarette. The air in the coffee shop was already faintly blue with second-hand smoke— there seemed something almost wholesome about pulling in a lungful of good, clean, fresh poison.

She squinted, releasing her smoke as if it were a mouthful of bitter words, and twitched her upper lip. Just like Humphrey Bogart. She stared up at the slowly revolving ceiling fan, and a tune began humming itself in her mind.

A man plopped into the chair across the table, breaking the mood. He wore a black t-shirt with a Roswell alien on it. His eyes were young, but his over-tanned skin looked weather-worn and the sun had bleached his blond hair to platinum. He would look, she thought, the same at 70 as he did tonight. Good news for him then, not so good now.

He grinned, showing many straight white teeth, and said, "You Ricky?"

She nodded.

"Funny, when we were chatting on the 'Net, I thought you were a man."

"So?"

The guy in the Roswell shirt shrugged. "So nothing. Just a comment."

"You bring the money?"

"Yeah. Ten brand new Franklins, just like you said." He pulled a #10 envelope out of a hip pocket and passed it across the table.

Ricky looked into the envelope, counted the bills, and slipped five of them into her purse, leaving the rest in the #10.

"Roswell" took a snapshot out of his other hip pocket and handed it to her. "His address is on the back."

The picture showed another man, maybe fifty; paunchy, baggy-eyed, smiling; iron-gray hair rimming a pink dome.

"Looks like a typical murder victim on America's Most Wanted," Ricky said, in a cynical drawl. "All the neighbors'll say, 'He was a great guy— do anything in the world for you.'"

"Roswell" laughed shortly. "Anything but die. Like I said on the 'Net: He's my father-in-law. Put some money in trust for the little Princess so no fortune-hunter can touch her capital. Put some in trust for himself, to see him through a good, long life. Meanwhile, he's spending everything else. If he keeps it up, there won't be anything left for me— for my wife to inherit. He dies tonight, and enough goes into her account that the interest can buy a trust-busting lawyer."

Ricky lit another cigarette and puffed her first draw across the table.

Roswell coughed and fanned the air. "Must you?"

"Yes."

The waiter brought the cappuccino and a stack of napkins with YAN-KEE JAVA stamped on them in flowing script. "Anything else? — Anything for you, buddy?"

"No, thanks."

Ricky sipped her coffee while Roswell fidgeted.

"So?" he said. "Have we got a deal?"

She nodded. "I'll make the arrangements now." Her glance flick-ered to the door, and she stubbed out her cigarette. She picked up her purse, the envelope, and the photograph.

Roswell didn't watch her leave. He didn't see her nod to the Yankee Java's owner, a large and handsome former movie actor. He didn't see her talking to a man outside the shop, handing the man the envelope, pointing inside to him.

After a moment, Roswell left. Just outside the door, he bumped into a man; a man who jammed a gun into Roswell's ribs and walked him around the corner to a gray van. The man glanced around, clubbed Roswell with the gun butt, bundled him into the van, and drove him away.

Ricky watched from the shadows, then returned to the coffee shop and her table.

"Your friend left," the owner told her.

"Well, that's the way it goes," she said. "One in and one out."

"Your coffee's cold, isn't it?" the waiter asked.

She tasted it and nodded. "I'll have another, please."

The woman who had called herself Ricky sat looking at the photograph of the intended victim. *A guy works hard all his life*, she thought, *—tries to do what's right by his family— and you might know a weasel would come along and try to muscle in. Lucky for guys like this*, she thought virtuously, *there are people like me looking out for them. I mean, crooked is one thing, but a person has to have some scruples.*

Fresh cappuccino came. She lit a cigarette, blew out the smoke, and lifted her cup to the photograph on the table.

"Here's lookin' at you, kid," she said.

Contributors

Marian Allen lives in a big house in a little wood, which is not the only difference between Allen and Laura Ingels Wilder. Allen has three novels on electronic disk (alternatively known as "coasters"), and has two novels currently being agented to paper. Wish her luck.

Jeannine Baumgartle writes poetry and fiction. Her work has appeared in publications such as *Green Meadow Press*, *Flying Island, Literally*, and Studio: *A Journal for Christians Writing* and recently won a residency for poetry at the Mary Anderson Center for the Arts . She and her husband live in the small town of Crandall with their two children.

Marla C. Bilbrey Since life is constantly changing, so does her writing style. Parent of five children and married to a husband with odd working hours, she has to be creative to find time to write. One of her favorite places is while sitting by her goats and horse, with the dog at her feet.

Ginny Fleming doesn't know the meaning of the word "Fear." The pages "F" through "G" are missing from her Funk & Wagnal. Credits include three optioned sitcom scripts, two movie scripts traveling on a slow train around Hollywood and a novel under consideration. She traces her roots to Milltown (Miller-Perkins) and leaves her heart in Sarasota.

Dirk Griffin Alas— we mourn the late Dirk Griffin. He was so late, he almost didn't make this book. If he was any later, we wouldn't have this bio— but we anticipated him. We wrote it anyway. Dirk is survived by unwilling family, a passel of friends, a gaggle of enemies, creditors and a plethora of nodding acquaintances. Dirk— we hardly knew ye.

Elizabeth J. Gross (nee Norwood) Known as Jeanne by her close friends. She finds time to write in the quietness of her home, while her husband, James, travels the waterways of the United States.

T Lee Harris lives in New Albany with a multitude of cats, three fish, one Chow-Labrador mix, one goat in a dog-suit and one humanoid housemate. Publication credits include illustrations and panel-to-panel comic strips in: *The Indiana University Southeast Student*, *The Huntingburg Herald*, *Fantaco's Spiderman Chronicles*, *Fantaco's Fantastic Four Chronicles* and various packages of shareware. T has completed a novel and is at work on the sequel.

Joy Kirchgessner is a business woman, illustrator and writer. Her paintings were recently on tour with the Kentucky National Art and Wildlife Exhibition. She shares her home with her husband and two horses.

Glenda Mills lives with her husband and two children in Floyd County. When she is not busy with homemaking and homeschooling, she writes fiction, nonfiction and poetry. She is presently working on her first fiction novel. Her first finished manuscript containing personal insights into the loss of a child due to miscarriage is presently on its way to various publishers.

The cover as it first appeared in 1998.

Previous Publications by
Southern Indiana Writers

Indian Creek Anthology
Ghost Writers
Christmas Bizarre
Dragon: Our Tales
Grounds for Suspicion
2000 Tales
Way Out West
Unbridled Lust
There's Something Under the Bedtime Stories
Novel Ingredients
Write of Passage
Off the Rack
Beastly Tales
It's Always Something

Coming in 2008

Most Wanted

Visit our web site for excerpts of previous publications
and availability information:

http://www.southernindianawriters.com